THE FATE

....

Priscilla Torres

Copyright © 2022 by Priscilla Torres

All rights reserved.

No portion of this book may be reproduced in any form without written permission from the publisher or author, except as permitted by U.S. copyright law.

Contents

Chapter	
1. *•. 01 .•*	2
2. *•. 02 .•*	8
3. *•. 03 .•*	14
4. *•. 04 .•*	20
5. *•. 05 .•*	28
6. *•. 06 .•*	35
7. *•. 07 .•*	41
8. *•. 08 .•*	48
9. *•. 09 .•*	54
10. *•. 10 .•*	60
11. *•. 11 .•*	66
12. *•. 12 .•*	73

13. *•. 13 .•*	79
14. *•. 14 .•*	85
15. *•. 15 .•*	90
16. *•. 16 .•*	99
17. *•. 17 .•*	109
18. *•. 18 .•*	115
19. *•. 19 .•*	122
20. *•. 20 .•*	131
21. *•. 21 .•*	138
22. *•. 22 .•*	145
23. *•. 23 .•*	152
24. *•. 24 .•*	160
25. *•. 25 .•*	167

1 9 year old innocent Eden was kept away from the world of 'evil' so everyone told her. After being kept away for 18 years Eden finally went into the outside world to explore what it's like, a year of exploring the outside that's when she meet them.

They changed her life, but she also changed theirs.

Azrael, Ace, and Ezra always did one night stands, never slept with the same women twice. They've also shared. They've been told they don't have a heart, always killed people in cold blood, the three friends grew up together since birth. Never let down each other, always got each other's backs, always shared, never let anyone get in between them.

What happens when they meet Eden?

Will Eden be scared of them because of what they do? Or will she still be the 'innocent' Eden everyone knows?

•. 01 .•

Eden's Pov-

The clouds look like cotton candy, which is yummy if you ask me.

I see a lot of things in the sky, that's why I love looking at it. Picturing different things, the color, the shape, the way it slowly moves. It calms me down

I wonder what it would be like to fly, i should jump off a plane- what if my parachute don't work and I die. Oh my god, than I'll be a pancake on the ground...

To busy in my world while looking up at the sky I didn't see the cars driving in front of me, until I felt an arm wrap around my waist causing me to look in front of me seeing there's cars crossing the road- the arm around my waist pulls me back like I'm a rag doll. Wee

Their touch makes me feel butterflies in my tummy-

Wait a damn minute, I almost got hit by a car, hm

"You should watch were you're going little girl" a voice came from behind me, startling me

I look down and see that the arm is gone, I pout at that, but I make this my chance to move away. Looking back I see three guys all glaring at me, what did I do?

"Why're you all glaring at me?" I give them my best glare, which causing their eyes to soften a bit

"You could've gotten hit by a car, if you weren't in your own little world." Says the man on the right side, he has black hair, and prefect jaw line, his eyes look like it's hazel. oh he's pretty...they all are

"You're pretty" I tell them, while smiling

"Hold on you almost die and the only thing you say is 'you're pretty'? Don't you even care that you almost died?" The one to the left says, his hair is brown and has brown eyes, pretty

"Oh no I know I almost died, which would've been a boring way to die if you ask me"

They all look at me with wide eyes as if I'm crazy

I look at them and smile, which causes them to snap out of it

"What's your name Tesoro?" The one in the middle asks me oh he speaks Italian, he has black hair and blue eyes, wow it's like the ocean, lovely

Isn't it lovely all alone?

Ah not now

"mi chiamo Eden Lilith qual è il tuo?" I reply, to which they look at me with wide eyes and open mouth

"Close your mouth before a fly goes in" I tell them and put my hand under their chin closing their mouth one by one

Still looking at me with wide eyes I ask again louder this time "What's your names?"

They snap out of it again, clearing their throats before speaking

The one in the middle speaks first holding out his hand, which I happily take "I'm Ace Mikaelson Darling, nice too meet you"

"Hello love I'm Azrael Hunter, it's a pleasure too meet you" Says the one to the right, and I nod shaking his hand

"And my name is Ezra Ronan, it's nice too meet such a beauty like you angel" he says, making me blush

The other two see me blush and glare him, what's up with them and glaring all the time?

"Where you headed?" Azrael asks me

"I was going to this new cafe, downtown. I've been hearing people talk about it" I tell him, debating on leaving or not

They all look at each other communicating with their eyes, cool, they all nod and look back me. I smile and wave

"Mind if we join?" Ace asks me

"Really?!" I smile feeling beyond happy, do they want to be friends?

"Yes, now show lead the way my lady" I smile and turn away to walk in the direction of the cafe

Is it weird that I'm going to a cafe alone with three guys? Yes.

Will I get probably get kidnapped? Yes again.

Do I care tho? No I do not, and that's okay, at least my kidnappers are pretty.

THE FATE

•*❁☽❁*•

•*❁☽❁*•

10 minutes later, we're here. Finally.

Oh this place looks niiiceee

"Oh let's go find a table" i say excitingly, while power walking like an old person, to which they smile at

Once we've all sat down, a waiter comes over

"Hello my name is James, I'll be your waiter today, what can I get you guys?" He says looking at all of us, stopping once he gets to

He smiles at me, Aw

"Ma'am what would you like?"

Smiling I order a Caramel Iced Coffee "Alright thank you beautiful."

I nod, and turn the other way so he won't see my red cheeks

Looking at the other guys, they're all glaring at the waiter causing him to shift slightly

"Um...what would you guys like?" He asks them nervously

"We'll like to have to have black coffee, thank you. You may leave now." Ace tells him sternly, the waiter nods and walks away. But not before glancing at me

They look back at me giving me a soft smile, I couldn't help but return it.

"So angel, how old are you?" Ezra asks me

"I'm 19 years old, how old are you guys?" They all look at me, than each other, looking back at me they smile

"We're all 27 years old. Eden would you like to be friends with us?" I smile widely, nodding my head rapidly. AHHHH I have friends! I HAVE FRIENDS!

"Yes, yes, yes, please. I'd love that very much thank you." They all smile at me, and nod

"Alright here are you drinks, would you guys like anything else?" A different waitress comes to our table, she's pretty, hm I wonder what happened to the other dude

They all look at me, asking me if I want anything else and I shake my head. All nodding at the same time, they turn to the waiter

"That will be all, thank you. Can I get the bill?" Ace asks

She blushes and looks down smiling

"Yes I'll come back, give me a sec." Turning around walking towards the counter, purposely swaying her hips

She has a nice body, wide hips, big butt, everything I ain't.

I look down at myself and frown, which didn't go unnoticed by the three

One of them puts their hand under my chin, making me look up. Seeing it was Azrael. Smiling softly at me, he comes closer to me and whispers in my ear.

"You're beautiful love, don't compare yourself to her. You're gorgeous." Feeling his lips graze my cheeks, causing me to blush, and they all chuckle

"So cute" one of them muttered

Sending butterflies to my tummy

•*~▫•*~▫•*~▫•*~▫•*~▫•*~▫•*~▫•

Hi

•. 02 .•

Third Person Pov:

Fuck

The three men, can't seem to get their minds off Eden. All their minds are all occupied with her.

They've met, a lot of women in their life time. None of who were real, they never showed their true self, it's always fake laughs, fake smiles, all they want is one thing from either the men and that's only sex. They never met anyone who's real, until her.

Seeing how free she was made something spark within them, they don't know what it is. But they crave more of it

After the three got home, they went straight to their office to get some work done.

30 minutes later

"Fuck! I can't concentrate." Ezra says running his hand through his hair

"I know me too, I can't stop thinking about a certain someone." Azrael tells both of them, while smirking

"I want her." Is all Ace said, because it's true, he wants her.

They all want her

Body and soul

"I'll call Jacob, and tell him to send us information about her. I want to see it all." Ace tells both of the others who nods in return

"Do you think we can stay friends with her? And if so, how long do you think we'll last?" Ezra asks

Thinking about it, we really won't last long Azrael thought. She's just so- I can't explain it.

"Alright I told him to send it to us when he's done, in the mean time let's try and catch up on some work. Lord know how long this will take, ah kill me already." Ace tells them, throwing his head back

"I volunteer as tribute!" Ezra says loudly while jumping out his chair holding up his right hand

Ace turns towards Ezra throwing a tissue box at his head while smirking.

"Ow that hit my eye you dumb nuts! Fight me bitch!" Ezra tell Ace getting into a fighting pose

Ace gets up and runs towards Ezra without giving him time to move, causing him to let out a girl yell. The fuck

THUD!

Azrael looks at the two of the them fall with the couch backwards. The only noise he hears is both of his best friend groaning lowly.

"Ow fuck first my eye now my dick?! Get the fuck off me you fat bitch!" Ezra yells out in pain

"You're the one who started this fucker." Ace replied

They both get up, stretching out their muscles, and dusting themselves off

Ezra turns to walk away, but Ace had other plans. Taking one step forward Ace he quickly puts his foot in front of Ezra causing him to trip falling face first into the carpet.

"Ow" Ezra groans "Ace I'm gonna call your mom, and tell her you're bullying me again."

Aces eyes go wide, looking to Azrael for help who's laughing wiping the tears under his eyes

Azrael stops and sighs, walking over to Ezra he helps him up "You okay man?" He ask

Ezra nods in return, sending Ace a glare he sticks his tongue out him, causing Azrael to chuckle

"How are you guys 27?" Azrael asks them

"I honestly don't know, we're like toddlers trapped in a grown mens body." They both say at the same time

•*❀ ☽ ❀*•

•*❀ ☽ ❀*•

Azrael was about to say something but got cut off by the sound of all their phones ringing.

Looking at their phones they see all the information about Eden that's their guy jacob sent to them.

State File Number:16300916292Name: Eden Rose LilithDate of birth: April 2, 2003, 19 years oldCity of birth: New York CityParents: Sophia Johnson Lilith (mother) November 21, 1968 Jospeh Collin Green (father) May 18, 1964Parents Status: Married Both Deceased (Car accident) December 3, 2020Mothers Place Of Birth: New YorkFathers Place Of Birth: MaineSchool Status: No RecordsSiblings: No RecordsRelatives: Sarah Kelly Smith (Grandmother)Home location: 27 Birch Ln, Redwood, Ny 12829Phone Number: (212) - 457 - 1890

Looking at the information sent to them, makes them disappointed

There's not the much on her, they all thought

"Hey Jacob, is this all you can find on her?" Ace asks with a hint of disappointment

Ace puts it on speaker for all of them to hear

"Yes sir, I've looked through all their family records, and checked their backgrounds, but didn't find anything. The only information I can find on Eden was the information I sent you sir." Jacob informs us

"Oh- alright thank you" Ace hangs up the phone and sighs

"Great, I guess we gotta do this the hard way. Not that I'm complaining, I mean look on the bright side we've got her number, we can hang out and ask a little about her." They all nod and add Eden's number to their phones

"Alright should we call her or-" Ezra trails off

"Yeah let's do it, I mean we only get one shot might as well take it." To which they all nod in agreement

"Who's doing it?" Ace asks both of them

"I'll do it!" Azrael tells them, pulling out his phone

His finger hovering over the call button, causing his heart to race.

Tap

The sound of the phone dialing, makes their heart rates spike. What if she thinks they're weird? Who'll she think we creeps? Will she even hang out with us?

All these thought rushing through their heads they didn't know someone picked up until the hear that beautiful voice that does wonders to them.

"Hello?" Her angelic voice saying through the phone

Not knowing what to say, they all freak out, eyes wide, looking at each other when no one speaks. Azrael throws the phone to Ezra, Ezra throws the phone to Ace, Ace throws it back to Ezra, and he throws it back to Azrael who looks at him with a glare.

Calming down, he clears his throat and speaks, putting the phone on speaker

"Hello love, it's nice to hear your voice. How are you?" He asks putting on a smile

"I'm great thank you for asking, but may I ask who's this?" They all frown at the question

"It's me love, Azrael. The one you went to the cafe with. Me, Ace, and Ezra were wondering if you wanted to go out with us for awhile."

They hear squealing on the other side of the phone, making them chuckle

"YES, YES, YES! Please, I'd love that. Where are you going? What are we gonna do?" She says quickly

"We'll do whatever you want to do darling." Ace says to her

"Yay! Wait....Will you kidnap me?" She asks and their smiles disappear, being replaced with a frown

"No Angel, we would never do that." Ezra replies

"Okay good, because that would be boring. Okay next subject. Can you guys pick me up at my apartment? I have no car, and we can go wherever."

"Yes, yes, we'll be there love. Text us the address, and let us know when you're ready. And we'll be on our way." Azrael says softly

"Alright, see you guys in a bit! Bye bye! TOODLES!" Eden yells the last part, making them all laugh.

This is gonna be fun.

•. 03 .•

Eden's Pov-

Five months later(A/N): I know, I know, far stretch

These past five months have been HEAVEN, I'm even joking. Ever since I've became friends with them Azrael, Ace, and Ezra they were really nice and patient with me.

Though sometimes I do get annoying at some points

Today we're going to the mall, good thing I still have money saved up to get a few things.

Everything is so expensive nowadays

We walk in, and they all follow behind me like lost puppies…hehe they're my b-

No Eden mama said not to say that

Buts she's dead, dead as hell

Shut up!

Walking past the Victoria Secret store I see underwear and bras on display, it's all so pretty, looking at all the girl walking in seeing they have a nice body for those underwear and bras hm

I wanna try

As I'm about to go inside, I get stopped by a hand on wrist.

Looking back I see Azrael scratching the back of his neck "Do you wanna go in?" He asks

"Yeah I wanna try on some or just buy some, they look pretty so I wanna go in. Can you guys come in with me? I don't wanna go by myself." Looking at them with puppy eyes, hehe

I've barley known they guys for a while, but I'm comfortable with them. They make me happy, and feel confident in myself I like it

"Alright daring, lead the way." Ace says, smirking at me...that does things to my tummy

"Okay, let's go!"

I walk inside and see all set of underwear, and bras. Wow! Mama never let me where these before, she says it for people who sin.

Cant live life without being a little sinful at least

"Hello Ma'am, I was wondering if you knew you breast cup size. If not you can hold you hangs up and I'll measure for you." She tells me politely, I nod and put my arm out

Wow this is awkward

"And you're cup size is an 36 D, you can look in this section and see what we have. Have a good day, let me know if you have any questions." She looks at the guys behind me and smiles at them, but they don't return it

Hehe

She turns on her heels and walks away

I look at the guys and they all stare at the bras and underwear, getting a basket I walk back towards them, and they start putting a lot of stuff in my basket, all different textures, designs, looks, and colors

Well alright than

"I think these will look nice on you" Ezra tells me "Everything looks good on you" he whispers to himself, I don't think i was supposed to hear that so I let it go

After looking around the store, and putting things in my basket were finally going to the check out when this group of girls walk up the the three guys behind me

"Hey handsome, are you single?" The girl with bleached blonde hair asks Ezra who keeps looking at me, now sparing a single glance at her

"Whatever you're not even hot anyway" she says

"What about you baby, are you single?" The girl beside her asks Ace, she has black hair and brown eyes

They still play attention to me, not looking their way. Making the girls mad and glare at me. One of them puts her hands on Azraels arm, and pulls his arm back glaring at her

"Don't touch me, and take a hint, we don't want to talk to you. And no we're not single, so please move along." He tells them sternly

After that they leave, when I go to pay for my stuff someone grabs me by the waist and holds me there

"You're not paying Angel, we are. It's out little treat you." I feel his breath on my neck sending shivers down my spine

•*✿ ☽ ✿*•

•*✿ ☽ ✿*•

Sitting in their office with them after we went shopping, they do work I continue to watch Friday the 13th on my phone. I only discovered these movies a few months ago, and I'm loving them.

I lay upside down on their couch that they have in their office waiting for them to get off. I like spending them with them here, it makes me feel safe and happy to know that we're all comfortable with each other

Looking at them I see them all looking at me and I smile, to which they return. Making me smile more, I like their smiles. It's pretty.

They all get from their seats and come to sit on the couch with me, yay!

"Hey Angel can we talk to for a bit?" Ezra asks me

"Yeah sure, what's up?" I ask while sitting back to normal, they all look like they're battling themselves inside their heads

"We wanted to ask you something." Ace says slowly

"We were wondering if you'd like to go on a date with us." Azrael tells me, with a looking of hope in his eyes

Us?

Does he mean all of three of them?

"Do you mean all three of you?" I ask confused

"Yes love all three of us, we'll go however slow you want. We just really like you." Azrael tells her putting his hand on hers, causing her to blush

She's thinking about it for a second, hm going on a date with all three of them?

It can't be that bad, I mean at least it ain't four people. I like them, and they like me. I guess we can work this out somehow

I look at all them and nod, giving them a smile

They all look at me with the most beautiful breathtaking- okay over dramatic but still they have pretty smiles. Pulling us all into a group hug, I can smell them

They smell goooooodddddd

"Can we get ice cream now? I've been waiting since we came back." The all laugh and let go

"Let's go than, what kind of ice cream do you want?" Ezra ask putting his arm around my shoulder

"I want cookies and cream, in a cone." He nods and we all make our way down to the parking garage

One time when I was small I had dream I was getting chased by big bird and that way scary!! I thought I was gonna get eaten by a fat chicken...wait is he a chicken?

We all make it to the car, get in and make our way to the ice cream shop

Shop....

I'll take you to the candy shop

"You okay their love?" Azrael ask from the drivers seat

"Yeah I'm okay, can we go now?" I ask impatiently

I want my ice cream!!

They laugh at me, but I glare at them. What's so funny? Food comes first, duh!

•. 04 .•

Eden's Pov-

After the guys dropped me off at my apartment, telling me they'll be here around 7, looking at my phone I see it's 5:45.

So I've got about an hour and 15 minutes to get ready, here goes nothing

Walking into my restroom I take off all my clothes, get in the shower and use my vanilla body wash. After that I use my coconut shampoo and lather that shi- no no no.

Anyway after doing my business in the shower I get out, wrap a towel around myself and put on lotion. I feel soft as a babies butt.

I walk into my closet and look at all the clothes i have. The guys bought me so many things, dresses, pants, shirts, bra, underwear, shoes, and accessories, I told them not to, but they did it anyway. Hm I wonder what I should wear. Thinking about what to wear I decided to go with a black silk dress. It only reaches my mid thigh.

I've never worn these types of clothes, but ever since I've tried it on in the store it made me feel pretty.

Mama and papa would never let me wear these. But they can't stop me now, so I'm gonna wear it.

I zip it up, put on my heels and go to the bathroom to fix my hair. I don't like tying my hair, it hurts my head, so I'll just leave it down.

I only put on mascara, since I don't know how to do makeup. I put on two necklaces, and earrings.

Looking myself in the mirror I feel beautiful

My phone dings snapping me out of my thoughts, looking at it I see it's the guys.

Aw they made a group chat with me

Azrael ♡'❏ꓴ❏'♡: Hi my love, we're here. Are you ready?

Me: Yes I'm ready, I'll be out in a sec | (• ꓴ•)|

Ezra (⊃❏•̀‿•❏)⊃: I bet you look beautiful Angel, just come on down when you're ready. No rush!

Me: Okay I'll be right there

Ace (ˇ ³ˇ)♥: Darling!

Ace (ˇ ³ˇ)♥: Darling!!

Ace (ˇ ³ˇ)♥: Darling!!!

Ace (ˇ ³ˇ)♥: Darling!!!!

Ace (ˇ ³ˇ)♥: Darling!!!!! Come on down already we miss you. Can't wait to see you, bye darling.

Me: Hahaha, I'm coming, I'm coming. See in you in a bit. ❏❏

🌑‿🌑 ❏❏

Smiling I put my phone in my purse, and make my way to the front door. Walking out, I close the door behind me, locking it and make my way to the elevator but get stopped by a voice.

"Hey excuse me miss" a unfamiliar voice says from behind me

"Oh hello, can I help you?" I ask the man who's looking at me up and down, making me feel uncomfortable

"Oh no, I was just gonna say you look hot. Wanna go on a date sometimes?" He asks me

No

"Uh no, no, but thanks for the offer. May I ask who you are by the way" I reply, making him glare a bit

"I'm your neighbor, I've been here for a year."

"Ah, okay. I'm sorry but no, I gotta go. It was nice meeting you." I turn and walk fast toward the elevator, getting in a let out a sigh looking down at myself

The doors open, and I make my way out

Spotting their car I make my way over there. Ezra gets out the back door and opens the passenger side, I get in and say thank you.

I look at them, only to see them looking at me with wide eyes.

"You look-" Azrael says but doesn't finish "You look so fucking gorgeous love, oh my god." He says whipping a hand over his face, making me blush

"Fuck Angel, you look beautiful." Ezra tells me, causing me to blush even more

"Darling, you look- God I can't explain it. I have no words" Ace exclaims looking at my outfit, with wide eyes

I probably look red as a tomato right now, oh god

•*❀☽❀*•

•*❀☽❀*•

After driving for what feels like hours we're finally here, it's an Italian restaurant. Cute

"You drive slow." I blurt out making my eyes go wide while looking at them

They all look at me seeing a smile creep up on their faces, Ezra lightly laughs while Ace is looking Azrael slapping his back twice.

Azrael smiles shaking his head getting out the car before coming around to my side opening the door for me, holding out his hand for me to take. Which I do.

Ace and Ezra get out too, and hug me, telling me how beautiful I look again. My heart!

They lead me inside and it's a nice restaurant, a lot of people in here. Must be popular, we make our way to what looks like an elevator the heck.

We ride all the way to the roof top, and what I see melts my heart. It's a small round table that how's candles and food on the top, and the view...Wow!

"You like it amore mio?" Azrael whispers in my ear, wrapping his arm around my waist. I only nod in return, not trusting my voice

"Come on Angel, let's eat." I sit down and they all smile at me

"I'm lost for words on how perfect this is, I love it. Thank you guys." Feeling my eyes water

"Anything for you darling, anything for you." Ace says giving my head a kiss

We all start eating, and talking about random stuff, and laugh at random things.

45 minutes later

Wow! That food was…so good, soooo good! Yummy now it's just sitting in my tummy

"That's was so good, thank you." I smile at them, and they return it. Aw

I get up and look at the view, a minute later I hear them walking towards the balcony looking down at the city

We all stand in comfortable silence until Azrael speaks up "Hey love, can we talk to about something?"

"Yeah." I nod, looking up at him

"Let's take a seat shall we?" We all walk over the bench, me and Azrael taking a seat, while Ace and Ezra stand looking at us

"We were wondering is you wanna be our-" He says looking a bit nervous

I give him a reassuring smile, he gives a small one back

"Will you be our girlfriend?" He says quietly I almost didn't hear him

I look up to Ace and Ezra, but they don't look at me. Only keeping their eyes down

They want me to be their girlfriend…does that mean they get to be my boyfriends?

"If I say yes, than you three will be my boyfriends?" They all snap their gaze to me, they all have to same look in their eyes, hope.

"Yes Darling we will be your boyfriends." Ace replied

"Imma ask again, will you be our girlfriend love?" Azrael asks

"Yes, I would love to be you guys girlfriend." A after I say that they all smile and hug me, squeezing me. I'm gonna fall over

"Okay I think that enough, we don't want to kill her." Ezra tells them pulling me into his chest, holding me there

"Okay if we're going to do this, we gotta have no secrets between us." Ezra tells me

"No secret? Okay." I smile into his chest, feeling warm

"In that case, I think we should tell her." Ace says making me worried

"Tell me what?" I ask slowly backing away from Ezra to look at all of them

"We're in the mafia, well actually we're the mafia but that's besides the point. We do things others wouldn't normally do, stuff we're not proud of, the world we live in is dangerous but we'll explain more to you later on. For now if you still want to be with us than you'll get dragged into this life. It's not easy, but we'll do anything and everything to protect you and make sure you're safe." Azrael stated, they all look at me seeing my reaction. But I just stand there looking at them

"The Mafia?"

"Yes Darling the mafia, do you know what the mafia is?" I nod slowly to his question

"Oh okay, I thought I was something bigger. But no, that's still cool though." I tell them and they look at me as if I'm crazy

"What?" I ask looking at them confused

"Nothing, nothing." Ezra says, snapping out of it clearing his throat

okiedokie

The other two snap out of it, and a softly smile at me. I happily return it. I walk up to them and hug them, making them respond quickly hugging me back.

"I have three boyfriends, yay!" I say quietly, they all chuckle

"Alright let's go Angel, it's getting cold." He takes off his jacket putting my arm in it.

We make our way down, and outside.

"Thank you guys for today, I really enjoyed it." I tell them and they all smile at me, causing my heart to beat faster

"You're welcome amore mio." Azrael says kissing the top of my head

We get in the car and make our way back to my apartment

40 minutes later we arrive at my apartment complex, damn already?

"Goodnight guys, I enjoyed our date. I'll call you guys tomorrow, goodnight." I hug each one of them, and kiss them on the cheek. Making me blush at what I did

"Goodnight love, be safe going up." Azrael whispers into my ear, he hugs me again, kisses my on my forehead

"Goodnight my gorgeous darling, text me when you're up in the morning." He kisses my on right cheek and sits back

Ezra squeezes through the middle and brings me into a bone crushing hug

"Sweet dreams angel, goodnight" He let's go, giving me a kiss to the left cheek, making me blush

"Alright goodnight" I get out their car and make my way up

As I'm about to go into my apartment someone puts their hands on my waist, making me stop and look back

It's the guy from earlier, my neighbor

"Please don't touch me." I tell him trying to push his hands off me I don't like this

"Come on baby, don't play hard to get." He smirks tightening his grip on my, pulling me closer to him. He puts his head in my neck, and tries to kiss me

Trying to push him away I head butt his nose, making him lose his grip on me. Walking up to him I push into the wall, kneeing him hard in his baby maker. Oops

Kneeling down he holds dick in one hand, the other holding his nose which is bleeding

"Oops sorry I slipped" I say feeling uncomfortable

Pulling out my phone I call the only people that make me feel better

•*❀ ☽ ❀*•

•. 05 .•

Azrael's Pov-

Sitting in the living room looking over documents, my phone rings right beside me. Looking at the clock it's 1am, I wonder who's calling me this late.

This better be good

Looking at the caller ID I see it's Eden, a small smile sits on my face while I answer it, "Hi my love"

"Azrael" I hear her small voice and I already know somethings off

"What wrong? Are you okay?" I ask getting more worried, hearing some a small whimper, I try to decide if I should go over there or stay here.

"Eden baby what's wrong?" Seeing the other to jog down the stairs, I stay focused on her

"When you dropped me off, this man...this man tried touch me. He made me feel so uncomfortable, I didn't know what else to do so

I just called you." I hear her voice breaking every second she spoke, it broke me

Someone tried to touch her? Fucking bitch is dead

"Alright I'll come and pick you up alright? I'll be right there love, don't worry." I tell her and hanging up the phone, standing from the couch I get my car keys, and walking out the front door, but ended up being stopped by Ace and Ezra

"Hey man where you going? It's 1am." Ace asks

"I'm gonna go pick up Eden, I'll be back" as I walk off I get stopped again, come on

"Eden? What happened to her?" Ezra asks looking worried, I drop my head looking down, letting out a sigh before looking at them

"She said someone tried to touch her in the hallway of her apartment complex, saying they made her feel uncomfortable. So I'm gonna go pick her up."

"I'm coming with you."

"Yeah me too, let's go."

I nod and walk back to the car and get in, the other two get in as well. And we make our way to her apartment.

45 minutes later we're finally here, getting out the car we all make our way to her apartment

Knocking on the door, we hear footsteps approaching the door until it finally opens revealing our girl still dressed the same as we left her

She looks up and her eyes water, running to hug us we all hug her back. Hearing her crying breaks us, after a few minutes she finally calms down.

I put my fingers under her chin making her look at us.

Red puffy eyes, my poor baby

"Darling what happened?" Ace asks whipping the tears off her cheeks

"This man tried to touch me, he approached me before I went down to meet you guys earlier. He called me hot, asked if I wanted to go on a date with him, but I said no. And when I got back from our date, he walked up to me and pinned me against the hallway and tried to kiss my neck but I didn't let him. And than he grabbed my waist and kept tightening his grip on me, and now I have bruises on my sides because of him." When she was finished she hugged Ace, and pushed her face into his chest trying to catch his breathe

"Alright darling, calm down. We're here, we'll take care of it okay?" Ace says, only earning a nod from her

"Do you know who he is?" Ezra asks her

"He said he's my neighbor, I don't know his name. But he has a bruised nose." She replied looking at Ezra who looks confused

"Why does he have a bruised nose Angel?" Being confused as Ace and me, he asks her

"I may have head butted him, and kicked his baby maker." She smiles

"There's that beautiful smile!" I say kissing her cheek, making her giggle. Her tears long gone

"That's my girl, good job." Ezra says kissing her forehead

"My strong girl" Ace says hugging her, giving her a kiss on the cheek

"Let's go, our angels probably tired." Ezra says earning a 'let's go' from Ace and me

•*❀☾❀*•

•*❀☾❀*•

45 minutes later

We're finally back home, parking the car in the drive way. I turn off the car and see my love looking at our house.

"Wow" she breaths out staring at the house with wide eyes and open mouth

"You guys live here?" She asks us, making us laugh quietly

"Yes amore mio we live here." I reply looking at her from the drivers seat

"It's beautiful! Let's go inside I wanna see how it looks." Opening her door and getting out quickly, this girl

We all get out, and walk up to the door and go inside.

"Oh my wow, it's even more beautiful inside!" She exclaims walking into the living room

Taking a seat on the couch we all sit next to her, she looks lost in her thoughts

•*❀☾❀*•

•*❀☾❀*•

Eden's Pov-

Will they get mad at me if I asked? I don't know if I should ask them, it's been on my mind the whole drive here.

"Are you tired darling?" Ace asks me, putting his hand on my shoulder

"No I'm wide awake, but I was wondering if you guy have something I can change into. I don't want to wear this dress any longer." I tell them, they all nod and get up from the couch

"We'll be back, don't move alright?" Ezra tells me following the other to, I nod in return

If they're in the mafia does that mean that they kill people? I've read about the mafia, I've heard about it over the last year.

I wonder if they do, if I ask how will they react?

I get snapped out my thought hearing footsteps behind me, assuming they came back already

"Here you go love" Azrael hands me a black sweatshirt that has a LV on the front...what's LV?

"Here darling" Ace hands me white fluffy socks, nice

"And here you are my Angel" Ezra hands me grey sweats

"Thank you guys, where the bathroom?" I ask

"It's just right under the stair right there, we'll be here when you come back. Just hand me your clothes and I'll throw them in the washer." Azrael tells me

"Okay." I happily walk to the bathroom, wow! It's a pretty bathroom, it's all black interior, marble counters, marble walls, oh my god

I quickly change into the clothes they gave me, and make my way out

"Here you go, thank you guys for the clothes." They all smile showing their beautiful straight teeth

"You're welcome love." Azrael takes the clothes and walks to I'm assuming the laundry room

Sitting back down on the couch I fidget with my hands

I wanna ask, it's bugging me. Deciding to just go for it I ask

"Can-can I ask you guys a question? You don't have to answer it's okay if you don't want to." I look up at them and they give a smile. Ace and Ezra come over and sit on either side of me

"It's okay Angel, don't be scared to ask us anything" He says holding my hand, caressing it with his thumb

I nod, and ask the first question that comes to mind

"Do-do you guys kill people?" I ask them, noticing how their shoulders tense up when I asked the question

"Yes angel, we do...kill people" Ezra looks at me nervously, waiting for my reaction

"Are they innocent people?" Their tense shoulders drop in relief, they smile softly at me, causing me to get butterflies again

"No darling, they're all bad people. We don't kill innocent people, never have never will only the bad ones." Ace tells me, kissing my forehead

"So...since you guys kill people can I kill people too?" I ask them innocently, causing them to all chuckle

"Do you want to kill people love?" Azrael asks me, with a look of amusement

•*❀☽❀*•

• *~▫• *~▫• *~▫• *~▫• *~y▫• *~▫• *~▫•

Hi.

This was kind of a longish chapter, but I hope you enjoyed it.

Please vote and comment, I'd love to hear your thoughts and stuff and stuff. ☐

Thank you all for reading my story thingy, I appreciate it. <3 I'll probably update two more times today. Since I've got nothing else to do.

I love you!

•. 06 .•

Eden's Pov-

"Do you want to kill people love?" Azrael asks me, with a look of amusement

"No baby, it's not for you." Ace smiles hugging me, giving me a kiss on my forehead making me pout a bit

Crossing my arms stubbornly "But I want to try pleaseee."

Giving them all puppy eyes hehehe

Ezra sighs and looks at me "Alright, if it makes you happy Angel, you can try. But we're warning you though, there's a lot of blood."

I happily hug Ezra really tight making him run of out air, it's okay though he'll survive. Letting go he gasps for air look at me with wide eyes, but I give him an innocent smile. Hehe

"Okay so when will I be able to try?" I excitedly bounce on the couch making them smile

"Soon love, soon." He says giving a small smile "Are you sure love? You're too innocent for this, I don't want you to be scared of us."

"I'm sure I'll be fine." I give them a big smile

Yay! I get to kill people

This is new, I like new. Only live once might as well, no one's here to stop me

"Alright we'll talk about this in the morning, for now let's go to bed. You'll be sleeping with one of us, and that's your choice to make. The other rooms are not done yet." I nod and look at all of them, but I want to cuddle with them all. I pout at the thought

"Ezra can I sleep with you tonight?" He looks surprised but agrees anyway. I look at the other two and see them smile, I'll sleep with them next time.

If I ever come back here, I hope so I like staying with them already

"Okay let's go up, come on Angel." Ezra says holding out hand for me to take, and I do obviously. Azrael comes up to me and hugs me

"Goodnight amore mio, I'll see you in the morning." He kisses my head and walks up the stairs

"Goodnight Eden darling, sweet dreams. See you in the morning." Ace hugs me and kisses my cheek, and goes upstairs as well

Ezra lead us upstairs after a few minutes of being in the living room

Once we make it up the stairs and go down a hallway, I see 5 doors, 3 to the left, two to the right

"Me and Aces rooms are on this side of the hallway, his room is a door down from mine. And aces on the right side of the hallway, right there. We don't have the other guest room ready." He point to the last door at the end of the hallway on right side, so his and aces room are on the left side. And one room separates them, hm alright.

"And here it is, my room." He opens the door and wow-

His room is pretty, the walls are different shades of grey, bed is big and comfortable, has a walk in closet by the bed, and lamps that give the room perfect lighting.

"I'll sleep down stairs okay? Let me know if you need anything" he tells me walking towards the door, but I stop him before he can go out

"Can you stay with me Ezra? Please" holding his hand tugging him to the bed

He nods and gets in bed after me, and wraps his arms around me, putting my head on his chest and wrapping my arm around his waist. I feel safe in his arms, as if nothing can hurt me. I want this to last forever.

After a few minutes of laying here, I fall asleep to the sound of Ezra's heart beat. It's peaceful

•*❀☽❀*•

•*❀☽❀*•

Ezra's Pov-

Seeing she's finally asleep, I slowly unwrap myself from her hold. Missing the warmth arlready

I didn't change my clothes because we had somewhere to go, it's 4am right now, so we gotta get going. I only spelt for two hours and 20 minutes so, here we go

Walking out the room quietly I go downstairs and see them waiting

"Took you long enough." Ace says impatiently

"Sorry I had to make sure she was actually asleep, now let's go." I tell both of them, walking to the front door

We get in the car, and drive to where we're headed

45 minutes later we arrived at her apartment complex, and make our way up.

Knocking on the door next to hers, it opens revealing a middle aged man. Looks 40 to me, old fuck!

Seeing his broken nose, makes me smirk. My Angel did that.

"What hell do you guys want? It's almost 5 in the morning?!" The man whisper shouts

As he's about to close his door I step in sending him a smile, while the other two glare at him

"Today you assaulted a girl, and that girl happens to be our girlfriend. So you know what I'm going to do to you for putting hands on something that belongs to us? I'm going to cut off every single one of your fingers, and than your ears go next, maybe your tongue too. Guess we'll have to wait and see." His face pales, and his eyes go wide. I smirk at him before glaring, stabbing a needle in his neck

He goes limp and falls backwards onto his coffee table breaking it, fat fuck!

"Alright let's get this over with, we'll go through the stairwell, and out the back. The cars back there." Azrael tells me and Ace

"Okay let's go."

We take him out the apartment, and walk to the stairwell dragging his body in a bag.

Once we reach the stairs we were 'tired' and we just decided to let him tumble down the stairs. He's like a tumble weed...a big tumble weed.

"Alright the cars right there, let's get him inside." We nod and put him in the trunk and get into the car, making our way back

•*❀☽❀*•

•*❀☽❀*•

45 minutes we arrive home and drag this fat fuck into the basement

Putting him in a chair, we cuff his hands on the arm rests and tie his legs to he legs of the chair. And PERFECT!

He'll be out for a few hours, so that's good.

It's 7am now, we make our way upstairs and go to our rooms to freshen up and surprise our Eden

Seeing she's still laying in bed hinging a pillow makes me smile, adorable

I take a shower get into fresh clothes, do skincare, brush my teeth and go to wake up my beautiful Angel.

"Eden wake up" shaking her lightly he groans softly

"Baby wake up, we have a surprise for you." I say kissing her forehead

She finally gets up, and looks at me "A surprise?" she asks

"Yes Angel a surprise, come on get up. Come down when you're ready, oh and don't shower. You can shower after you're done with your surprise okay?" She nods half asleep, I tap her thigh twice getting off the bed walking out the room, giving her space to freshen up.

This should be fun.

•*❀☽❀*•

• *~▫• *~▫• *~▫• *~▫• *~*▫• *~▫• *~▫•Hi.

Those of you who are still here from the first chapter, thank you for the reads. I love you! <3

Thank you @annaannyyaa10 and @luxury2006 for the votes :3

I'll probably update again before I go to bed, which would around 3:00am because I have a hard time sleeping so yuh. Look forward to another update in a few. :)

Thank you for 230 reads. ♡

Muah! (˘ ³˘)♥

•. 07 .•

 Warning this chapter contains torture in it x

Eden's Pov-

Ezra left the room, leaving me to alone. It's okay I gotta go freshen up, but no shower? Really?

Walking into the restroom it's so pretty! All the interior in this house is unbelievable.

I grab the spare toothbrush brush from the cabinet, get toothpaste. And brush my teeth, yay no more morning breath.

I wash my face next and make my way downstairs.

A surprise? I wonder what it is, I can't wait.

Ezra left out black sweats and a black long sleeve shirt for me, thankfully. But why black?

Walking into the living room I see Ace, Szra, and Azrael sitting on the couch talking. I take a seat beside Ace who pulls me into a nice warm hug.

"Good morning darling, how'd you sleep?" He kisses my forehead and looks down at me smiling, I return the smile and kiss his cheek

"I slept good, thank you. How'd you sleep?" Returning the question to him

"I slept great, thank you." Letting me go, Azrael reach's across the table kissing my right cheek before sitting back down

"Good morning amore mio, you ready for your surprise?" Raising a brow at me, but I can see the amusement in all of their eyes

"Yes I'm ready, what is it?" I ask excitedly

"It's in the basement, and we'll take you there. Just to be safe we're not gonna eat breakfast until you're done with your surprise, because we don't want you feel nauseous or anything." He replies softly giving me a smile

"Okay, we'll let's go!" I get up, and I let them lead the way

Are they going to kill me? MaybeIs that okay? Totally fine because they're hot

We finally make it down the basement, looking at the walls it's all concrete, nice. A few door along the walls, leading to rooms god knows where. We stop in front of a door and they all turn to me with a worried expression on their faces.

"Angel just let us know when you want to leave, and we will alright?" I nod still confused

"Here goes nothing." Ace says holding my hand walking in the room, at first the room is dark. But Azrael reaches over and turn on the light, lighting up the whole room.

THE FATE

The first thing I see is a man sitting in a chair, tied up. He looks familiar

"Wake him up" Azrael says, and Ace throws a bucket of cold water on him. Causing him to jolt awake, gasping for air

Looking around his eyes land on me and the three men behind me making his eyes go wide, his face turns pale, and his eyes show fear. I feel powerful right now.

I like it

"W-w-what do you want from m-me?" His eyes showing panic, scanning all four of us

"A little recap for you, you touched our girlfriend, made her feel uncomfortable, and you didn't stop when she told you to. So now we're going to kill you." Azrael says sternly, making me shiver. It's kind of hot though

WHY HAVE I BEEN TALKING LIKE THIS LATELY?! oh yes it's my boyfriends who are making me like this

'So now we're going to kill you.' Azraels voice rings in my head

I snap my attention to Azrael who's grinning down at me. "Wait...Is he my surprise? Do I finally get to kill someone?" I try not to scream of happiness

Why should I be happy? IM KILLING SOMEONE!

I don't know, but i am happy.

"Yes you're going to kill him baby, go however fast or slow you want. It's you're first time make it special." He kisses my cheek, I jump on him wrapping legs around him squealing

"Thank you, thank you, thank you. Oh this is gonna be fun." I get off of him, and look at Ezra and Ace who are grinning at me

"Go ahead Angel choose what you want to use on him first." Ezra whispers in my ear, I turn a smile up at him

•*❀☽❀*•

•*❀☽❀*• ⚠

Walking over to the man, I smile happily at him. "Be glad you're my first, you're special."

"Remember this is what you for touching someone without consent." I smirk at him

Dragging the blade from his right arm, around his neck, and back onto his right arm. Hearing his breathing quicken makes me smile

"Baby, do you have a idea of what you want to do?" Ace asks me with a curious expression

Hm I have one thing in mind, once thing that I want

His heart

I smile and nod "Yeah I know what I want"

They don't bother asking, any mor questions. Letting me continue

Walking back over to the table that has tools I grab a small sledgehammer, cute. Turning around I see the fear in his eyes making me laugh a bit.

"This is going to hurt a little bit okay? So just sit tight for me." I tell him

Bringing the sledgehammer up, I slam it down on his ribs

One

Two

Three

CRACK!

Hearing his screams and whimpers is like music to my hear, i should not be doing this. But it makes me feel happy, and makes me feel powerful.

I love it

On the 10th hit on his ribs he's barely awake, spitting blood getting on my shoes. Ew

Throwing the hammer somewhere, I walk to the sink and get a bucket of cold water. Throwing it on him, immediately waking up. I turn around and look at the table once again

I try to decide if I want a knife or a meat cleaver

I think I'll go with the knife, it's pretty big. Has a pink handle, and the blade is black. Making my way over to him i open his shirt revealing his chest.

The guys start walking over to me with a glare on their face, but I raise my knife to them and point it to the chairs in the corner. Telling them to sit down, and let me finish

They are hesitant at first, but go and sit on the chairs watching me.

I smile at them and blow them a kiss, before turning back around to my special person for today. Groaning in pain, I bring my fist up and hit him three times in the face making more blood come out his mouth and nose.

Woah, I don't know where that came from. I feel like a 'badass' so people say

"Shut up, before I make this a slow death for you. And it will hurt, just so you know." I whisper in his ear making him shiver, making me smile at him

I bring the knife to the middle of his chest and press down hard making him yell, dragging the blade down at the way to his stomach I see all his blood pour out of him. Some of his intestines fall out of his body

Seeing he's still here with us, thank god I dig my hand into his body feeling all his warm and slippery organs I find his ribs and break them more. Hearing the crack makes me smile even wider, I'm surprised he's still a little conscious.

Fat bastard!

After break two more ribs, I slide my hand up to his heart and palm it. Making him look at me with wide eyes, feeling his heart rate beat poorly against my hand. Meaning he's about to die now, I grab that thing and rip it out his chest.

Seeing the life drain from his eyes

That's satisfying, the way it leaves there body

Looking at his heart in my hand, and my clothes that have blood on it. The floor that has pools of blood on the clear plastic laid out, I smile.

Yay! I killed my first person I'm so proud of myself

That was fun 10/10 would do it again.

I turn around and see the guys mouths open and wide eyes, holding a shocked look on their face. What?

"Look I have a heart!!" I jump excitedly snapping them out of daze. They all smile proudly at me, and walk up to me.

But not before pulling the front of their pants, they look uncomfortable

The all kiss me on my cheeks and forehead telling me how proud they are. I feel loved and cared for, I want this forever.

With them

•*❀☾❀*•

• *~▫• *~▫• *~▫• *~▫• *~*▫• *~▫• *~▫•Hi.

I hope you enjoyed this chapter. <3

Wow I updated about four times today, that's a record. Kk toodles!

•. 08 .•

Aces Pov-

Holy fuck

That was hot, I'm not even going to lie and say it wasn't because it fucking was.

I look at Azrael and he looks uncomfortable, motherfucker got turned on. Well we all did. Seeing her covered in blood, and killing him was just so-ah!

Are we weird for getting hard while watching a girl killing someone? Yes

Do we care? No because Eden and she's fucking gorgeous

Right as we look at her, we see her smiling at us holding a heart in her hand.

I honestly thought she'd be freaked out of all this stuff, especially the blood and guts. But I guess not, that's my girl.

We get up and walk over to her "I'm so proud of you, that was amazing for your first time. Are you okay?" I ask her worried she might freak out about what she just did

"I'm okay, are you okay?" I smile and I nod "Yes I'm okay darling, let's go get you cleaned up shall we?" Nodding her head we make our way back up

"Get someone here to clean this shit up." Azrael tells the guards

We all walk to our rooms, because of the blood on us from touching Eden. But I don't mind Deciding to take Eden to my room to shower, we go inside and she looks around.

My room has on grey colors, I like that color.

"Wow you have a cool room, why's your bed middle of the room space thingy?" Looking at me confused

I walking up to her smirking "It's there, so it can't make any noise." I whisper in her ear making her shiver

She looks at me still confused but let's it go

"Okay the bathrooms over there, you can take a shower I'll leave some extra clothes on the bed for you. And don't worry I'll shower in the guest bathroom." I tell her walking into my closet I grab the extra clothes for her and me, putting hers on the bed, I grab mine and make my way to the guest bathroom

Looking down I see I'm still hard from earlier, fuck. I guess I'll have to rub one out

•*❀☽❀*•

•*❀☽❀*•

Looking around his bathroom I see things for skincare, well at least he takes care of his skin.

I'm in love with his bathroom, it's so pretty!

I go back into the bedroom and get the clothes he left for me, and walk back into the bathroom. Stripping out of my bloody clothes, I throw it into a trash bag, and walk into the shower.

The water is hot, making all my muscles relax. I love hot water, the burning feeling against your skin when the water hits it.

I sigh and stand there for a few minutes, relaxing.

Looking around I see his body wash and shampoo, thank god it's not a 3-in-1 shampoo, and body wash.

Oh this looks expensive, oh well might as well enjoy it while I can.

45 minutes later

After getting all the blood off me, I wash myself and get out. That was a relaxing shower, except for the smell of blood. Ew

I smile remembering what I did, I killed someone. My first kill

I put on the clothes after putting on lotion, and walk out the bathroom. Only to be met with Ace sitting on the bed. His head snap up and meeting his eyes, I smile.

"All done darling?" He asks making me blush

"Yes all done, what time is it?" I ask looking for a clock

"It's 10:27 come on the guys made breakfast." Kissing my cheek he grabs my hand dragging me down stairs, I'm met with the sweet smell of food. Yummy!

"Goodmorning my love" Azrael says putting a stack of pancakes on the table. I run up to him and hug him, he kisses my cheek making me blush

They see my cheeks, and chuckle

"Where's my hug angel?" Ezra opens his arms, making me smile

I run up to him and jump, he catches me putting his hands under my thighs while laughing

"Goodmorning my beautiful Eden" he kisses my forehead, and I return it. Pulling back I see his cheeks light pink, making me smile more

Oh yes food!

I get off him and make my way to the table and eat. Moaning at first bite, this is good

"Mmm this is so good." I look at them and they all shift looking uncomfortable again

"Are you guys okay?" They all snap out of it and nod taking a seat at the table and start eating

Hm weird

•*❀☽❀*•

•*❀☽❀*•

It's now 8pm and I stayed the whole day at their house watching movies or talking about their mafia and stuff. It's pretty interesting

Right now I'm laying on Azraels chest watching death proof

"Eden?"

"Hm?"

"I was wondering if you want to stay her for the rest of the week" he tells me, making my eyes go wide

A whole 6 days with them? Yay!

"I'd love too" I smile up at him and he smiles kissing my head I feel special and safe

2 hours later

It's now 10pm and we're going to sleep, though it's a bit early for me. I don't mind if I'm with them.

"Who's room do you want to stay in? You can stay in Aces and than mine tomorrow night." Azrael tells me, walking up to aces door, hm going to sleep with Ace tonight and than Azrael tomorrow, that don't sound bad.

So I nod at him "Alright I'll sleep here tonight and than with you tomorrow." He nods

"Goodnight love, sweet dreams. He's already inside, waiting so you can just walk inside." He kisses my head, and I kiss his cheek "Goodnight" I tell him and go inside

I see that Ace sitting up against the headboard, hearing my footsteps he looks up and smiles.

Holding out his arms, I walk over to him hugging him. He grabs me and pulls me so that I'm straddling him. I blush at our position making him smirk

What's up with these guys and smirking?

I look in his eyes down to his lips and back up to his eyes, seeing he is staring at my lips. Making my heart race

He leans forward, making me lean in as well

Feeling his breath hit my face I lean in more, his lips look soft. I wanna touch it

Closing the space between us our lips meet, causing my heart to beat faster, feeling tingles all over my body

My first kiss

His hands feel hot on my waist, his grip tightening making me gasp

Our lips start to move in sync, me following his movements. I tug his back hair making him groan. Oh

The kiss gets heated quickly making me lose track of time, just than I feel something hard underneath me poking my thigh

•*❀☽❀*•

• *~▫• *~▫• *~▫• *~▫• *~*▫• *~▫• *~▫•Hi.

Sorry I've been busy with school, I'm a senior. I just hope I graduate this year.

What grade are you in?

And thank you all for the reads and votes. :) 600 reads! Ahhhh

I'm writing chapter nice right now, so yeah. Except it in a few hours

I love you <3

•. 09 .•

⚠️ Warning this chapter is a bit Steamy in it x

which was shit if you ask me, anyway enjoy! This not so steamy scene

Eden's Pov-

Feeling something like the inside of my thigh I move against it making him groan. Oh

His grip on my hips tightens while pulling away from the kiss "Don't do that Eden" he tells me, making me want to do it again

And I do

Moving my hips down more, I feel something down there that sends electric sparks throughout my whole body. It fees good. Trying to get more friction I love my hips against his, both our centers touching.

Grabbing the back of my head he kisses me more roughly than the first time. His tongue sweeps across my bottom lip trying to part my mouth, but I don't open for him making his groan into the kiss.

Putting both of his hands on my 'ass' as they call it. He squeezes it with both hands making me moan, taking this opportunity he pushes his tongue into my mouth. Both of us fighting for dominance. Of course he won

He groans when I pick up pace, putting a more firm grip on my hips, he moves my hips in a circular motion making me feel sparks again.

Gripping his hair in a tight grip making his moan. Oh

"Fuck baby" he says squeezing his eyes tightly, mouth open a bit

Hot.

I move my hips against his more and more, trying to find a release. I gotta release something.

•*❀☽❀*•

•*❀☽❀*•

Ace's Pov-

Fuck fuck fuck fuck fuck fuck

This feels so good, the way she's grinding her pussy against my cock making both of us hot. And her moans, god he moans, sound like heaven.

Putting on hand on her perfectly round ass, I put the other on her back making her arch, putting her beautiful round breast in my face.

Fuck

Moving my hips up to meet hers she gasps at the feeling, both of lost in pleasure. Our moans and groans are the only thing I hear. Pulling her into a more heated kiss I start to kiss down her neck, sucking, and biting.

Grinding her hips more he throws her head back, letting out strings of moans, putting me on edge.

"Ace I can't- this feels to good." She whimpers putting her head in my neck, gently sucking, and biting. Fuck that feels good.

The way my name rolls off her tongue gets me more hard, I can't get enough of it. Looking at her face, her eyes are closed, mouth open, lips swollen from kissing roughly, face flushed and she's breathing fast. Damn she's hot

Kissing under her ear trying to find that sweet spot, once I find it she whimpers, not enough. I bite it gently, making her let out a loud moan. Thinking she moaned to loud, she bites her bottom lip trying to counsel her noises.

Bringing her head down to mine I pull her lip out from the between her teeth and kiss the hell out of it.

"Don't hide your moans from me piccola ragazza you got it?" I mumble against her lips, gently nipping it

Moving her hips back and forth more against mine, she whimpers lost in the feeling.

I grab her hips and pull her more against me. Her chest touching mine, but not once did she stop moving her hips.

"I said do you understand Eden darling?" She nods her head rapidly "Words little girl."

"Y-yes daddy." FUCK

And that's what pushes me over the edge "Fuck Eden" I say her name over and over, like some prayer.

THE FATE

But let's try not to bring something holy into the unholy...like right now

Her hips start moving faster against mine, her pussy rubbing my cock through our clothes making us closer to the edge.

Squeezing her ass more I groan, throwing my head back.

"A-Ace I'm starting to feel something." She tells me, holding my shoulders, digging her nails into 'em

Shit

"It's okay darling, just let it go. It'll make you feel better." I tell her feeling the familiar build up in my cock. Her hips putting her pressure on my dick, I moan into her neck

She moans loudly before releasing, me following right behind her. Biting her shoulder to counsel my moan.

I cum hard, emptying myself the euphoric feeling, like I'm on cloud nine.

Both of us trying to catch our breath from come down from our highs. We lazily move our hips against each other riding out our orgasm together.

I grab the back of her head and kiss her lazily but soft and gentle. She moans when I squeeze her ass, I guess she likes that.

Pulling away for a breath I look at her, seeing hickeys on her neck and some bite marks I smile. "My beautiful baby, you did good."

Remembering what we just did her face turns red, hiding her face into my neck. Making me laugh, while holding her.

Rocking us from side to side I pick her up and take her to the bathroom , sit her on the counter and turn to turn on the shower.

Walking back out I get her clothes for both her and I, returning to the bathroom I give her clothes and kiss her forehead.

"Take a shower in here, and I'll go to the guest bathroom alright?" She nods and kisses my check making feel a whole ass zoo in my stomach

"Okay, I'll be in bed if you're not back in time." She tells me, I smile and nod, turning around I walk out the restroom and the room, making my way to the guest bathroom

•*❀☽❀*•

•*❀☽❀*•

30 minutes later

I get out the shower freshly showered, put my clothes on, which is only boxers and sweats. Sleeping with a shirt on is uncomfortable, so I like sleeping with a shirt off.

Free the nipples!

The fuck where'd that come from?

Brush my teeth and make my way back to the room quietly.

Walking into my room I throw my dirty clothes in the hamper and make my way to the bed. Seeing my beautiful girl is already sleeping I slip under the covers, bring her closer to me. I'm touch deprived already

I kiss the top of her head and she mumbles random things under her breath making me smile.

"Goodnight baby" I whisper against her head, giving it one last kiss I turn off the light by the bedside and cuddle with my girl. Letting sleep take over me

•*❀☽❀*•

• *~▫• *~▫• *~▫• *~▫• *~*▫• *~▫• *~▫•Hi.

Sorry I thought I uploaded this chapter but I didn't which sucks ass!

I don't think I'll be able to graduate this year, which sucks. It's to much for me, my mental health is getting bad again, I have four days left, and at least 100 assignments due. I didn't do shit, than my families gonna start talking shit, but all I can say is that I tried. But they ain't gonna understand, and that gets me mad. Anyway yeah, how's y'alls life?

This ain't that steamy, but I'll try again next time.

Hope you enjoyed this chapter! :))

Oh yeah thank you all for 1.02k reads!!! AHAHSJDJAJAHXHCHDJSJHAYALL ARE THE BEST

Toodle, I love you! ♡'▫‿▫'♡

•. 10 .•

Eden's Pov-

Waking up to the sun hitting my face made me groan, why is it so freaking bright?! I look around and see I'm not in my room, but in Aces room. Flashbacks start coming back from last night, making me blush hard.

We did that- omg!

I CALLED HIM DADDY!!!

Gosh I hope he doesn't remember that part. But last night was...I have no words. I never knew I could feel like that, it felt like I was floating.

Snapping out of my thoughts I feel myself needing to go pee. Oh no!

Getting off the bed, I get pulled back by a heavy arm around my waist pulling me back to his chest.

"Don't go." He mumbles in his morning voice, that's hot

I sigh and try to get out of his hold again, but he tightens his arm around my waist.

"Just 10 more seconds please." Putting his head further into my neck, giving it a light kiss.Making me blush I probably look like a tomato oh lord.

"I need to go pee." I tell him shyly

He immediately lets go, and telling me to go. And that he'll be up in a bit.

Walking into the bathroom I look in the mirror and my eyes widen at the sight of my neck. Marks all over my neck, all different sizes, shapes, colors. What do they call these again? Hickeys? Yeah hickeys.

He gave me hickeys.

I blush for the tenth time this morning and do my business, once I'm done I walk back outside to see Ace at his closet getting clothes out. Noticing me standing here, he looks up and smiles at me. Putting the clothes down, he walks up to me, and grabs my chin kissing me.

"Don't worry I brushed my teeth in the guest bathroom, and Goodmorning baby." He says kissing me once more

"Goodmorning Ace" I say shyly

He sees my neck and smirks, making my face so red. I look down and see his neck and oh my!

It's like mines, hickeys and bite marks.

Now I'm got to admit...he looks hot with those on his neck.

"And you look fucking gorgeous with my mark on you too darling." He tells me kissing my neck slowly

"Alright change your clothes, we'll all be in the kitchen okay?"

"Okay" I look anywhere but him, feeing my checks warm up. I really said that out loud!

He chuckles and kisses my head one last time before walking out leaving me to take a shower.

•*❀☽❀*•

•*❀☽❀*•

Walking down stairs I see all the guys around the island in the kitchen, making breakfast.

They hear my foot steps and look up at me, smiling. Azraels eyes go to my neck and he smirks, and looks at Ace so is smiling cheekily while putting a strawberry into his mouth.

Ezra walks up to me and kisses my cheek mumbling a 'Good-morning my sweet Angel' against my head

"Good morning Ezra, how'd you sleep?" I ask him, giving him a kiss on his cheek

When I'm done, I see Azrael bending down to my height, turning his head to the side making me smile and kiss his cheek.

"I slept pretty good, how'd you sleep?" Ezra asks from beside me, he sees my neck and smiles, looking at Ace and Azrael who are smirking as well making me blush

"I slept good thank you very much, good morning Azrael" He return the good morning and kisses my forehead

Looking at the food on the table, I lick my lips, oh the food looks yummy!

Ezra looks at where I'm looking, and laughs grabbing my waist, he pulls me to the island, and pulls out a chair sitting me down in it.

"Eat my love." Azrael tells me, I take a bite out of the pancake and moan at the taste. God this is heaven

I look up to say something, but their eyes are all on my mouth. And their gaze darkened a bit.

What the-

•*❀☾❀*•

•*❀☾❀*•Ezra's Pov-

Fuck she looks hot, I have a hot girlfriend. And those hickeys Ace gave her fuck she looks so fucking gorgeous gah damn!

Snapping out of it, I walk back to my seat, and start eating my food.

Mm I wonder what we should do today

"Hey Angel what do you want to do today?" I ask her while getting up for more strawberries

"Um I don't know what do you guys want to do?" Shes asks us, but we want to do whatever she wants

"We're asking you love not the other way around." Azrael tells her

"Can you guys teach me how to shoot a gun? If that's okay with you guys." She quickly adds on, we all look at each other a smile

Turning back to I say "Yes Eden that's okay with us, we'd love to show you how to shoot." I smile at her, making her bounce in her seat

Cute.

•*❀☾❀*•

•*❀☾❀*•

"Okay so remember you hold it like this, and when you need to reload you press that button there and it comes out. Than you put another magazine inside and shoot alright baby? You got this." Ace says giving her a kiss

A KISS!!

I mean I'm not surprised, because Eden has hickeys...well they both do but they kissed?! Nice, good for him!

Eden takes her spot in front of the target and shoots, bullet come flying out the gun landing on the floor with the other shells.

She looks hot shooting a gun, she can shoot me and I'd say thank you.

When the last bullet shell falls out the chamber it lands on her arm, making her flinch from the hotness of the bullet.

We quickly walk over, inspecting her arm. I give it a kiss and look at her to see she's blushing.

"I'm okay, it doesn't hurt anymore. Just caught me by surprise is all." She reassured us, we give her a worried looked but nod

She smiles shaking her head, getting on her tippy toes she grabs my head and kisses me. Shocking me.

Backing away she moves onto the other two and kisses them, making their eyes go at the small gesture. "I'm okay, you guys don't have to worry. But thank you for caring I really appreciate it." She tells us, we aren't really paying attention to what she says but we all nod

SHE KISSED ME!!!

She blushes and goes back to the gun, taking out the old magazine, and putting a new one in shooting again. Leaving us all shocked still, her lips were so soft my god!

She's going to be the death of me

•*❀ ☽ ❀*•

• *~▢• *~▢• *~▢• *~▢• *~*▢• *~▢• *~▢•Hi.

Sorry I haven't updated, someone was in my house around 4:50am. I was still awake at the time, just keep in mind that I live ALONE. So yeah I've been busy, I tried telling the cops, but they ain't doing shit. So there's that. Fucking cops.

Y'all I'm writing another book called All Alone, and the first chapter is out now. I wrote the other chapters but I'll wait on those ones.

Anyways hope you had a great day/night! And hope you're okay. <3

Toodles, and I love you!

•. 11 .•

 Warning this chapter is a bit Steamy in it x

Eden's Pov-

It's currently the last day I'm here at their house, and it makes me sad, I want to stay here with them longer. But I don't want to intrude to much time.

We mostly spent our time in the house of in the garden, nothing much. The only time we went out was to go to target, or to get some food around 2 in the morning because I was hungry. They made my life easier, and I've been more happy than I've been in my whole life. I can express how much I'm grateful for them.

Over the past week I've been here with them, I've become more open to things. And one of them is cussing.

Yup, I'm starting to cuss more often and it's a unhealthy problem if you ask me. Hey in my defense I only cuss when something happens, or I feel frustrated and what not.

Right now I'm laying with Azrael in bed, clinging to him like a monkey.

Last night I slept with Ezra, i basically take turns sleeping with them. They don't seem to mind, so it's all good.

"Hey beautiful what are you thinking about?" Azrael asks me moving so he's hovering over me on one elbow looking down at me

"All three of you guys made these pass months the best time of my life, I can never repay you for all you guys have done for me, I'm forever in you guys debt. So thank you for all you guys have done." I tell him quietly, feeling my eyes stinking with unshed tears. They make me feel safe.

He looks at me with of adoration, making me feel butterflies. Leaning in he kisses me slowly, I immediately respond. Wrapping my arms around his neck, he leans down more.

He breaks the kiss and looks down at me with lustful eyes, making me squirm a little under his hot gaze.

"I know a way you can repay me little one." He whispers in my ear, gently nipping my ear

"W-what would that be?" I curse myself for stuttering

"Do you trust me?" He asks me, I nod back in return it really trying my voice. "Words baby"

"Yes" seeing he's satisfied with my answer he tugs at my pants

Pulling away from me, he grabs hold of my pants and pulls it down my legs slowly along with my underwear. Making my breathing quicken

⚠⚠⚠

He grabs my ankles spreading my legs open, my pussy on full display for him making him groan.

I've never shown a man or anyone my private areas growing up, and he's the first to see it. Thank god I shaved this morning! He looks hot.

"Such a pretty pussy, my god!" He groans quietly, making my heart rate pick up again

Oh lord

•*❀☾❀*•

•*❀☾❀*•

Azraels Pov-

Slowly pulling her pants and panties down her soft legs I finally see what the fabric were hiding. Spreading her legs more I see what I've been waiting to see.

Lord give me strength, because this girl is going to be the death of me.

So pink, looks soft, such a pretty pussy that looks like it's never been touched. "Such a pretty pussy, my god!" I groan quietly to myself, not caring if she heard me or not. Even if she did hear me, I didn't lie. Because it's so- ah!

Staring at it, I see her arouse slowly dripping out of her sweet cunt.

"Here give me you hand love." I tell her reaching out to take her hand "I want you to show me how wet you are for me." Telling her softly, I see her confusion at first but it's quietly replaced with a shocked look, she nods and brings her fingers up and down her slit with my help, fuck if that didn't make me cum-

Moving her hand more confidently she whimpers, removing my hand from hers I watch her please herself. Feeling my dick get hard even more At the sight of her.

Getting closer to her I can smell her arouse making my mouth water, wanting to taste her more.

She quietly moans at the feeling, hearing how wet she is I pull her fingers away from where it was and bring them to my mouth. Slowly sucking on it, keeping eye contact with her.

I moan at the taste of her on my tongue

Grabbing her thighs I spread 'em more for me, gripping them tightly in my hands. Licking slit, I get lick her clit gently biting it. With this action her hands immediately go to my hair gripping it tightly, keeping me in place.

"Azrael." She whimpers as I continue to torture her clit, licking, biting, sucking.

Eating her like a starved man, and I am...For her pussy.

I bring my hand to her entrance, teasing her. I gently push one in making her hips buckle, back arching off the bed.

So fucking tight

This view is fucking hot from down here, she's hot.

Waiting for her to adjust I push up her shirt to reveal her breast, Jesus! Moving my fingers in and out of her sweet cunt slowly, I'm graced with her beautiful hot sexy moans making me even more hard than I already am.

I lick her clit one last time before getting up taking one of the nipples in my mouth while I continue fingering her.

"Fuck you taste good." I exclaimed

She moans in return, moving my fingers faster inside her, her hips rising off the bed. But I press down on her lower stomach, making her moan even louder.

Kneeling down again I grab her thighs and continue to pump my finger into her going down to lick her sensitive clit.

"Don't stop, please!" She whimpers pulling at my hair more causing me to groan. That feels good, oh I'm not going to stop baby. Don't worry. "Please."

Thrusting my fingers more harder into her, curling them making her gasps and pant trying to catch a breath. "Azrael fuck! Oh God, Oh fuck!" She cried out, her body shuddering, I suck on her clit more trying to over power the pleasure for her.

Trying to move away from my touch I groan, and pull her back to me. Putting her pussy in my face even more.

Her pussy clenching around my fingers with her climax washing over her. I groan when she cums, getting more of that sweet taste that I craved for. I lick every single drop, not wanting this moment to end, I've never tasted a more better pussy than hers. God I'm lucky!

Thank god for sound proof rooms, because her moans belong to me tonight.

I remove my fingers from her and she lets out a small whimper, making me smile. My good girl.

Bringing my fingers up that have her cum on it up to her mouth, she looks at me with wide eyes.

"Suck them." I demanded

She closes her lips around my finger and sucks them clean. My dick pressing against the fabric of my boxers wanting to just be inside her already, feeling how warm, and tight she is. Feeling how her pussy stretches around my cock, taking me all in. Inch by inch slowly.

Shaking my head I get rid of those thoughts, great now Im stuck here with even harder and raging boner, that's waiting to be touched. But I won't do it, not tonight, so I guess I'll just sleep it out. Even though it's uncomfortable, this night was about her, not me.

"You did amazing baby, I'm proud of you." I tell her kissing her making her taste herself on my tongue. She moans and tugs on my hair pulling me more into her.

"That felt good." She mumbles quietly against my lips giving me a smile

"I'm glad I made you feel good love. Now let's get you cleaned up." I say, picking her up bridal style taking her to the restroom running a warm bath for her.

⚠️⚠️⚠️

•*❀☽❀*•

•*❀☽❀*•

I wash her, do her skincare shit. And put my clothes on her, and we go to bed.

And yes I did change the bedsheets and shit.

Holding my beautiful girlfriend in my arms I kiss her head and close my eyes. Replaying all that's happened today.

•*❀☽❀*•

• *~▫• *~▫• *~▫• *~▫• *~*▫• *~▫• *~▫•Hi.

Hope you enjoyed the smut, I tried! :,)

Don't forget to vote, comment, and follow. Oh and don't forget to share! <3

I love you all, toodles!

•. 12 .•

Eden's Pov-

We're currently sitting in the living room of my apartment, Aces is laying between my legs, Azrael is sitting behind me, with his arms around my waist, and Ezra is sitting beside me, with his head on my shoulder.

We're watching final destination, love these movies.

They didn't want to go just yet so they decided to stay for a while.

"I'm gonna order food, you guys want anything?" I ask making them look at me

"No we're okay." They all say, I nod and get up off the floor making them groan

"Come back" They say holding out the hands, making grabby fingers. I laugh at their behavior, walking into the kitchen I sit on the counter and call the Chinese Restaurant that's down the street.

"Hello thank you for call The Best Sichuan, how can I help you today?" The lady over the phone says

"Hi I was calling to make an order." I reply, seeing Ezra walk into the kitchen he sees me and smirks

Walking over to me, he puts his hands on my knees pulling them apart so he can step in between it.

"Okay what would you like to order?" They asks me but I'm to busy paying attention to Ezra who puts his head in neck and gently sucks, making me let out a breathy moan

"I-I would like steamed dumplings, and beef stew please." I tell her trying to control my voice and breathing.

He licks my, and bites it making me squirm. This feels good. He starts sucking again, occasionally kisses my neck. His hands on my knees go up higher and higher, I move my neck to the side giving him more space making him smile.

"Alright, would this be Pick up, or would you like to have it delivered?" She asks me

Claiming down i say "delivery please, thank you."

"The food will be delivered, and you can pay when it gets there. Thank you for calling, have a nice days" I hang up the phone and grab onto Ezra hair pulling it making him groan

He backs away from my neck and looks at it, giving me a smirk.

I pull him in by the shirt and kiss him, his tongue running along my bottom lip asking for permission. I open my mouth and he slides his tongue in making me moan.

Putting my legs around hiss waist I bring him closer, both our centers touching each other.Kissing him hard, I bite his lip, and gently suck on it making his grip on my thighs tighten.

I smirk and pull away, looking up at him I smile and push some of his hair that fell down back into place. Giving on last kiss I gently push him back, and walk back into the living room with Ezra not to far behind me.

"Finally! Did you order your food darling?" Ace asks me, I nod and sit back down.

They immediately engulf me in a hug, making me feel safe. I love this

•*✿ ☽ ✿*•

•*✿ ☽ ✿*•

"The food's here, the front desk has it. I'll be back I'm going to go get it." I tell them, they tell me to be safe, to which I return with a nod

Great I've got to take the stairs, it was just working bro what the fuck.

Walking to the elevator I see a sign on it 'Close for maintenance' I sigh and walk toward the staircase

I'm almost at the end of the stairs, after walking and walking. Food here I come!

Hearing footsteps I don't pay attention to it thinking it's people who live here, as I'm about to open the door to the lobby someone grabs my waist and puts a cloth over my mouth and nose.

Trying to fight the person off, I slow down starting to see black dots cloud over my vision.

And finally the darkness consumes me.

Ace's Pov-

As I'm waiting for Eden to get back I start to get this bad feeling, as if somethings about to happen.

I look at Ezra who's on his phone looking down at it, I see his eyebrows furrowed until his eyes go wide in a panic

Jumping up from where he sat on the couch he runs to the door opening it before running down the hallway. Me and Azrael look at each other with a confused look.

We get up and run after him closing the door behind us, we see he's going toward the stairwell.

"Ezra what happens?" I asked worriedly once we catch up to him

"Eden got taken, someone took her." He says quickly

So that's what he was looking at on his phone, the cameras in the stairwell, he was looking after her. He seen what happened to here, I swear to god I'm going to kill whoever took her.

Me and Azrael look at each worried about her, we rush down the stair. Once we get down there we see nothing other then her phone on the floor.

"Son of a bitch!" Ezra yells picking up her phone

Fuck one of us should've gone with her, and this wouldn't have happened.

"Let's go, we can look at all the cameras. Call Jacob tell him to search the area, you and Ezra go to the front desk ask if they seen the man that took her. And I'll go back up to get our stuff, let's all meet up at the car once we're done." Azrael says, trying to remain calm

Both Ezra and me nod, and go walk out into the lobby and go to the front desk. While Azrael goes the back to the apartment to get our stuff and make a call.

"Hi how can I help you fine gentlemen?" Says the lady behind the desk, batting her lashes

"Yes we were wondering if you seen this man around here, like 5 minutes ago." Ezra tells her pulling up the picture showing her

"Oh him yeah, he was here a few minutes ago. He left with a girl, poor thing looked sick.." she says looking at the picture with a pout

"Do you know which way they went and what kind of car they had?" I ask

"Yeah the went straight into the downtown area, and they were driving a black Chevrolet Cruze I think that's the name. It had a sticker on the back window. That's all I remember, why do you ask?" She asks looking at us suspiciously

"We're undercover cops and we were tracking him down, thank you miss for your time." I smile forcefully at her

Turning around I pat Ezras shoulder and we make our way to the parking garage. Seeing Azrael leaning against the car we get in and drive to the house

This fucking person has a death wish, don't worry Eden we'll get you back.

•*✿☽✿*•

• *~□• *~□• *~□• *~□• *~*□• *~□• *~□•Hi.

So I was gonna release some chaphter if my second book, I don't know if I should but. No alot of people read my stuff, but I'm thankful for you all that stayed this far! <3 I love you

Vote, Comment, Follow, and Share :))

Bye, toodles!

•. 13 .•

Eden's Pov-

I'm awoken by ice cold water being spilled on me, why cold?

"Look she's awake." An unfamiliar voice says

I try to pull my hands up to wipe my face but they won't move. Opening my eyes slowly, the lights blind me making me squint. Looking around I see I'm in a basement kind of place, it's clean, so it probably ain't used that much or never.

"It not going to budge you know?" The same voice tells me, stepping closer, I look up and see- oh he's ugly

"Yeah I figured, so tell me why am I here?" I ask calmly looking at them waiting for an answer

"You're here because we need information about the trio that you got comfortable with, and you're the only one who's close to them. If not I'll kill them, or maybe I'll kill you." Mr.Ugly Balls says giving me a ugly smirk, gross

"I mean what's to tell? They don't even tell me anything, I don't know anything about them, eveytime I'm with them they ask all the questions, they don't give me a chance to ask one. So there's that." I lie

"Thought you'd say that." He walks over to me and slaps me across the face

My head turns to the other side, feeling that stinging affect on my cheek makes me smile.

Smiling I turn to him looking him dead in the eyes "You hit like a bitch." I say laughing slightly

They two men looks at each other and walk out, leaving me all by myself. They really thought I'd be scared? Please, what's there to be scared of?

I sigh and think about what my three Angels are doing right now, I miss them. Hopefully they find me soon

•*❀☾❀*•

•*❀☾❀*•

The door opening wakes me up from my beautiful slumber, IT WAS GETTING TO THE GOOD PART!

Looking at the door I see a new guy walking beside Mr.Ugly Balls, he has a weird ass looking hair cut, motherfucker looking like lord farquaad. Walking around like there's a stick up his ass.

"Hello Eden you don't know me so let me introduce myself. I'm-" I cut him off"You're lord farquaad, I know." I tell him, he gives me a confusing look

What?

"Who the hell is lord farquaad?" He asks me

"He's from Shrek, you know Shrek, Fiona, donkey...No?" Oh this poor man don't know who Shrek is, that's sad

Shrek is love, Shrek is life

"What the fuck- Anyway I'm Leon, I want to know where they are staying. We can't find their address, it's like they're ghost. And you're the only one who knows where they are. So where the fuck are they?" He hissed getting into my face

Ew coffee breath

He sighs and looks at Mr. Ugly Balls who gives him a tablet, scrolling through it he smirks.

Showing me the pictures, I see it's me. Walking, doing laundry, eating, sitting on the bench in the park. "You're obsessed with me? I don't know what to say, thank you? Though I am flattered, I have someone special in my life already sorry." I faked getting flustered

"This bitch- no! We need information or else you won't like what happens!" He yells in my face

"Sorry I don't know shit." I lie, looking him in the eyes

"She's giving me a headache." Mr.Ugly Balls says pinching his nose bridge. "I'm going to kill this bitch, she's getting annoying."

"How long have I been here?" I ask

"A day and half, you didn't wake up when we knocked you out. We tried to wake you up, but you didn't, so we poured water on you for the third time and boom! You're awake!" Lord farquaad tells me

"This is boring." I sigh closing my eyes

"Oh you just wait, we have a surprise for you. Than you won't be bored anymore." He grins touching my cheek with his sausage fingers

"Don't touch me with your sausage fingers, hot dog lookin ass fingers. I'm not scared of you, try me you fucking pussy! Oh and I'll be waiting." I exclaimed giving him a smile

"You bitch!" He yells about to hit me, but doesn't get to because of gunshot sounds ringing throughout the place.

FINALLY!

•*❀☽❀*•

•*❀☽❀*•Azraels Pov-

"Anything yet?" I ask Ezra who's typing on his laptop furiously

"No nothing yet, I ran his face to see if anything pops up but nothing. I can look at all the cameras to see what turns they took, but if they went out the city than we're on our own." He tells me, not once looking up from the laptop

"Fuck." I say quietly, I hope she's okay. She's been missing for a day and a half and I'm getting more worried and scared for her

"Yeah, yeah, just do that." I tell him, sitting on the chair next to him while he works

1 hour later

"GOT IT! I FOUND HIM!" Ezra yells, me and Ace looking up from our laptops and run over to Ezra

"That's where she is, this guy named Leon Brown and his crew took her. They're here, it's just 10 miles out of the city. The house is registered in his mothers name Lisa Brown." He says quickly showing us the place, it looks like any normal house. The fuck-

"What are we waiting for come on!" I tell them, walking to my room I get my gun, put it in my pants and walk out.

Going to the weapon room, we get what we need and make our way to our girl.

We're coming love don't worry.

"Call Jacob tell him the address, and to bring some men with him. Right now." I tell Ace while getting in the car, he nods and gets out his phone calling Jacob

1 hour later we finally get here, we get our guns and make our way inside shooting anyone that gets in our way

Gunshots ring through out the whole house

Getting to the last door I see my girl, she's here. But she has a knife to her throat, seeing the guy behind her, or he's ugly...

"Let go of her right now!" I yell pointing my gun at him, Ace and Ezra come in as well pointing at him

"I'm going to kill her right now." he says putting his hand on her waist making her glare

"I told you not to touch my with your ugly ass Vienna sausage fingers you wild ass looking lord farquaad bitch! Let me the fuck go!" Eden yells grabbing his arm and flips him over making him land on his back.

Grabbing the knife she stabs his right eye making him scream, stabbing his left eye he finally passes outs. She digs the knife into his mouth curving it upwards until it looks like he's smiling.

That's our girl

"I warned you bitch!" She says patting his chest twice before looking up and running to us engulfing us in a warm hug

"I was waiting for you guys, how'd you guys find me?" She asks smiling up at us making my heart beat faster

"Ezra did most of the work, we were looking at CCTV footage and all that stuff." I tell her

She looks at Ezra smiling at him, he smiles back with a bigger grin.

"I would kiss y'all but I'm covered in blood, so I can't. Thank you guys for coming here." She says

Even though she's covered in blood she still looks hot!

"Well let's go home shall we?" Ace asks making room so Eden can pass through, she happily walks in front of us

"He's ugly." She says walking pass a dead corpse on the floor

My crazy girl

•*❀ ☽ ❀*•

• *~▫• *~▫• *~▫• *~▫• *~*▫• *~▫• *~▫•Hi.

I don't know what to put so yuh.Hope you enjoyed

Toodles, I love you! <3

•. 14 .•

Ace's Pov-

As we drive back to the house I'm holding Eden in my arms, poor baby's tired. Tucking her head into my neck more I kiss her head.

Seeing the house come into view I gently wake Eden up "Darling we're home." I say softly

She quietly groans and mumbled something I can't quite make out

She gets out the car, and we follow after her making our way inside the house. "I'm gonna go take a shower okay? I'll be right back." She tells us we all nod but I say "We're all covered in blood, I think we should all take a shower. I hate the smell of blood, but the sight-" I cut myself short and grab Eden's hand gently and take her upstairs to my room

"Did he do anything to you?" I ask sitting her on the bed, she shakes her head and mumbles no. But I see a handprint on her cheek shaking he hit her, I'll just wait until she's ready to tell me.

"Well he slapped me, other than that nothing else." I nod getting up I walk into the bathroom and run a hand towel under cold water, folding it I walk back out to her.

Sitting beside her I gently grab her chin making her look at me, I put the cold hand towel on her cheek and hold it there for awhile.O nce I'm done I see it's not that red anymore, making me sigh in relief. I kiss her cheek and than her lips.

"You shower in here and I'll shower in the guest room." I tell her getting some clothes ready for her not wanting her to see how pissed I am. She nods and walks into the bathroom with the clothes.

Walking out the room, I see the other two walking up stairs.

I go over to them, standing in front of them i say "She said that she got slapped, but other than that they didn't do anything else."

Both giving me a black expression, but once the words processed in their brains their eyes go wide.

"The motherfucker slapped her?" Ezra asks me, I nod in return

"Yeah she has a handprint on her cheek, but I put a cold towel on it. So it should probably go away in a few days. Said that he hits like a bitch." I smile at the last part

They sigh in relief knowing it ain't that serious "As long as she's okay than I'm okay. Son of a bitch is lucky he's dead, or else I would've killed him myself." Azrael says we all nod in agreement

"We all look like shit, especially you Ezra." I tell them

"Oh sucks my dick, you look like shit you too bitch." Ezra says looking at me seriously making me and Azrael laugh lightly

"Alright you guys go take a shower, I'm going to the guest bathroom to shower. See you guys in the morning." I say, they nod and say the same

I sigh and walk to the guest bathroom, deciding I'm going to take a cold shower. The motherfucker slapped her, to bad he's dead.

•*❀☽❀*•

•*❀☽❀*•

30 minutes later I finished my shower and walk back into the room only to see her pulling the shirt over her head...no bra

I mean some woman that I met say that sleeping with a bra on is uncomfortable, that sucks. Cant be me, y'all stay safe tho.

She turns and jumps in fright making me smile "Sorry darling, I didn't mean to startle you." She smiles at me walking over and pulls me into a hug.

I immediately react and do the same. My teddy bear.

"You okay baby?" I ask tucking a strand of hair behind her ear, she nods yes. Even tho I wanted to hear her voice I don't push it.

She looks up and kisses me making my heart beat out of my chest. The kiss is soft, and sweet, I pull away to look at her and she looks at me.

Going in I kiss her harder this time, more intensively. Forcing my tongue in her mouth I groan at the feeling of my tongue hitting hers. Grabbing the back of her head I turn her head to gain more access, she moans at the new angle. Fisting my shirt, she pulls me more into her.

Our tongues battling for dominance, I won obviously.

Slowly pushing her to the bed the kiss gets more heated, both of us out of breath only pulling away for air and going back in.

Gently pushing her on the bed I look at her, seeing nothing but lust and adoration in her eyes. Mines probably look like that

She reaches up palming the back of my head, running her other hand through my hair, making me sigh at the feeling.

"I'm ready" she says quietly I almost didn't hear her

I quickly open my eyes and look down at her, only to see her smiling

"Are you sure? Baby you got kidnapped and now you want to have sex- are you sure?" I ask, she gives me a weird look and turns her head to the side probably feeling embarrassed

"Baby I just want to make sure the time is right, I don't want you to feel pressured into anything." I tell her gently pulling her chin so she's looking at me

"May not be the best time, but I'm ready. And if you don't want to do this than that's okay, I understand. But just know that I trust you enough to give you my body, and once I do that you better take care of it." She says calmly looking up at me, I smile at her words.

She trusts me

That's all I need to hear...I nod but ask for the last time "Are you sure?"

She smiles showing her prefect white teeth, she nods "Yes I'm sure, I want it to be you Ace." She says almost shyly making my heart beat crazy

THE FATE

I lean down and kiss her, taking her bottom lips in mine I sigh and the feeling on her fingers trailing up my chest, over my shoulders, and down my back.

I grab the end of her shirt and look at her for consent, she nods and I take it off

Holy fuck!

So round, more than a palm full. Nipples hard from the cold air, her perfectly flat stomach. My mouth waters just looking at them.

Fuck she's killing me!

•*❀☽❀*•

• *~▢• *~▢• *~▢• *~▢• *~*▢• *~▢• *~▢•Hi.

I ordered books, but the bitch didn't even come in the mail. And they asked if I wanted a refund, so I said yes. And they only gave me $5 back. And they whole thing costed $41, bro what the fuck!

Anyway that's all. Thank you all for the votes I love you. <3 it mean a lot!

Vote, comment, share, and follow! <3Follow my socials if you want to. :))

Oh sorry to keep you waiting ;)

Toodles, I love you!

•. 15 .•

 Warning this chapter is a bit Steamy in it x

Eden's Pov-

⚠️⚠️⚠️

He lifts up my shirt slowly and just stares at my boobs with lust.

Licking his lips, he goes down taking one nipple into his warm mouth making me moan arching my back. Putting my nipple into his mouth more.

He gently bites 'em causing my hand to fly to his hair tugging making him groan.

He sucks, licks, bites, and kisses it making me go crazy. Feeling my pussy clench onto nothing, I need a release.

After giving both of them attention he slowly goes down until he's eye level with my covered pussy. Looking up at me through his hooded eyes he asks for consent, I nod and he wastes no time pulling my underwear off.

"Cazzo, dammi forza" he says quietly under his breath making me squirm under us heated gaze

"You're going to cum for me three times, be a good girl and do that for me okay la mia bella troia?" He asks bringing out his thick Italian accent

That's hot

"si signore." I tell, he grins up at me and goes back to what he was doing

Licking my slit he groans and I arch my back, buckling my hips more into his face. He grabs my thighs and squeezing em tightly

"cazzo, hai un sapore così buono, piccola." He continues licking my clit, making me moan loudly.

Trying to move out of his grip the pleasures too much. Too intense. My breathing becomes labored, as I try to catch my breath. But it's hard when he's sucking on my clit. My hands tugging at his hair making him moan into my pussy, my walls clench around nothing making it hurt.

He doesn't stop though, only tightening his grip on me. Dragging his tongue through my folds again, eating me like he's dying.

Sucking on my clit hard, making me see stars dance before my eyes, right before the pain turns into pleasure.

Putting one finger into me I arch my back, moaning. Slowly thrusting it in and out of me, after a few seconds he adds another finger making me clench around his fingers.

Latching onto my clit again he licks at a fast past, looking down at him I see he's looking at me and smirks.

I throw my head back and take both my breasts into my hands kneading them. Reaching up he takes on boob in his hand and massages it, squeezing my hard bud in his two fingers.

Picking up his pace, he thrust his fingers faster into me putting me on edge.

Curling his fingers again hitting my g spot he takes my clit back into his hot mouth and gently bites it making me go over board.

I moan loudly as I cum on his face, he groans lapping up all my juices like a starved man. Giving my clit a final kiss me come up and kisses me, making me taste myself. I moan at the taste, tugging his hair.

"That felt good." I say breathlessly making him chuckle

"You taste good, fuck you looked hot from down there." He says sucking on my neck, moving my head to the side to give him more space.

Kneading my breast he gives me one final kiss before saying "One down, two to go." with a smirk.

Laying down he grabs my hips and puts them on each side of his head, making me hover over him. "Why are you hovering? Sit." He demands tugging my hips down until my pussy is in his face, dragging his tongue across my already sensitive clit I moan, reach down to grab his hair.

His tongue goes to my core and slides it in and out, I move my hips against his face making him moan. As I ride is face he squeezes my ass in his hands kneading both of them.

Sucking on my clit my hips buckle against his face "Too sensitive, too sensitive." I says breathlessly closing my eyes

"Sorry baby." He says kissing my clit

Going back in he lick my slit making my legs start to shake around his head.

Moving my hips he mumble "There you go baby."

Putting one finger in he finger fucks me until my legs shake even more around his head, feeling my orgasm creeping up on my I moan loudly

"Are you close darling?" He asks, I nod in return. "Words Eden."

"Yes, yes I'm close-fuck I'm cumming!" I tell him gripping his hair riding his face faster

One last lick to my slit, I cum on face for the second time making him moan. Grabbing both of my thighs he pulls me down more he begans cleaning me up with his tongue.

"So fucking good" he mumbles against my clit, kissing I gasp, he kisses my inner thighs both sides. "Two down one more to go la mia bella troia." He tells me

Finally my legs give out and I fall to the side next to him breathing heavily.

"Dovresti cavalcare la mia faccia più spesso." He says giving my neck a kiss before reaching over to the bedside table and pulling out shinny black wrapper

"Are you sure baby?" He asks while holding up the wrapper in his hand

"Yes I'm sure. I need you now please." I say desperately

Smirking he says "This is a condom, so you won't get pregnant. We use this during sex, so it won't happen. Okay? I told you because you were giving this a weird look." He says laughing lightly

"Okay, so we use a condom?" I ask curiously

"Yes darling we use this, I don't want you to get pregnant right now since you're young and you still have some things to learn." He says smiling softly

"Okay you ready?" He asks, I nod. Giving me a reassuring smile he settles in between my legs putting my feet on the bed opening my leg for him more

Taking off his pants and boxers he's fully naked in front of me. God he's fucking hot!

Looking at his dick- shit that's big...how's that going to fit inside me?!

"Bro I'm tiny as fuck, how would that fit? You see how small I am? You're going to tear my in half my guy!" I exclaimed looking him in the eyes

He laughs leaning down to kiss me for a few seconds and pulls away leaving me breathless

"It's okay it'll fit, just let me do the work. You just chill there okay?" He says smiling down at me "You're beautiful baby, thank you for trusting me." He tells me after a second goes by making my heat skip a beat

"It's going to hurt a bit, but since I made you cum twice already I should just slide right in. I'll be gentle alright?" He asks me kissing me a few times

"Okay, I'm ready whenever you are." I tell him giving him a soft smile

Tearing the condom open with his teeth he takes it out and slides it on his dick and gets into position

He moves his hips forward, I feel his dick poking at my entrance. I clutch onto his shoulders looking at him in the eyes with adoration and love

Sliding into me more "così fottutamente stretto" he says closing his eyes, his breathing picks up

Feeling like I'm getting torn in half I squeeze my eyes shut, his movements stop immediately "Baby it's okay, just breathe, relax and breathe okay? Just look at me." I open my eyes dragging my gaze all over his face, beautiful is all I can think.

I lean up to kiss him and he kisses me back. His movements continue, pushing more into me I look down and-

Oh god

•*❀☽❀*•

•*❀☽❀*•Ace's Pov-

Seeing her looking down at where we're connected her eyes go wide Shit.

Grabbing her chin gently catching her attention I say "Don't look down there, you're okay." She nods in return

After I'm in my breathing is heavy and my eyes are droopy

Fuck she's still tight even after what we did, I thought i would be able to slide right in. But no.

The way her walls clench around my dick makes me feel like I'm in heaven.

Stopping my movements I wait for her to adjust and once she gives me the signal to start moving I waste no time in doing that

Moving my hips slowly I lean down and kiss her trying to distract her.

After a few thrust she breaks the kiss and moans into my mouth aching her back. Seeing pleasure take over her features I pick up the pace.

"cazzo, cazzo, Eden." I repeat over and over again

"You feel so good." I tell her putting my head into her neck, her nails dragging down my back creating a burning sensation. Putting me on edge

He legs wrap tightly around my waist pulling me closer to her

"Faster Ace, please." She begs

And her wish is my command, I move my hips more and more faster. As I go deeper into her, she moans loudly hugging me into her.

Sucking one of her nipples into my mouth I bite it making her groan, kneading the other one I pinch it between my fingers. Rolling the bud gently, before doing the same to the other side. Seeing hickeys on her breast I smile in satisfaction.

I reach down and play with her clit, pitching it making her clench around my cock in a tight grip. Fuck!

Feeling her pussy throb around me, I can tell she's close. The room being drowning by our skin slapping, moans and groans making us more hot.

"Are you about to cum Eden?" I ask her putting my forehand against hers

Nodding she leans her head into my neck and starts kissing, moving my head to the side she bites me making me groan.

Sucking on my neck she kisses it, before looking at it and smirking.

FUCKING HOT

Feeling the familiar build up in my cock I thrust more into her tight heat.

A few more thrust late we both cum while moaning into each other's mouth. Feeling her cum around my cock felt like heaven, emptying myself inside the condom I collapse onto her, being careful not to smush her.

"That was amazing." She tells me giving me a kiss

We kiss lazily, I pull back "You did good tesoro. You came three times, good job baby." She blushes and hides her face in my neck making me laugh lightly

"Are you okay?" I ask, she nods her head

We stay here for awhile with me still inside her softening, I pull out of her slowly making her hiss. "Sorry darling." I say giving her forehead a kiss

"It's okay, I'll be sore tomorrow. But it was all worth it. Thank you for being my first Ace." She tells me making my heart jump

I smile at her "come on let's go get cleaned up." Taking her to the bathroom take off the condom, tie it and throw it away. I run a bath and let her sit inside while I go back to the room and change the sheets.

After doing that I go back into the bathroom and get inside the tub with her.

Her back to my front, we just lay there in each other's arms for awhile.

How did I get so lucky?

⚠️⚠️⚠️

•*❀☽❀*•

• *~☐• *~☐• *~☐• *~☐• *~*☐• *~☐• *~☐•Hi.

What's up with y'all only reading the smut, and not the other chapters? SMH

This was kind of a shit written smut because it was her first time. So yuh!

Anyway hope you enjoyed, look forward to more in the further. ;)

Don't forget to vote, comment, follow, and share | (•‿•)|

Thank you @_letttuxxx for the votes! I love you (⊃☐´‿•☐)⊃

Toodles, I love you! <3

•. 16 .•

⚠️ Warning this chapter is a bit Steamy in it x

(A/N): Not y'all skipping the other chapters and only reading the mature ones, yeah I see you. (ಠ‿ಠ°) why do I even bother...anyway-

Eden's Pov-

"No don't wake her up." A voice says waking me up

"Come on man she's got to eat, it 12 o'clock already, why is she even sleeping this late? Usually she's up around 7." Another voice replies

It's quiet for a few seconds until "Dude why is she this tired?" A voice I recognize as Ezra's voice says

"She...we...uh stuff I don't know." Ace tells them

"Hold on don't tell me...you guys-" I cut Azrael off but me yawning and opening my eyes, squinting at them because it's fucking bright as shit in here

"You guys are loud." I tell all of them, they all give me some weird look- weirdos

"Hey darling are you okay? Anything hurt?" Ace asks me quietly giving me a worried look. I shake my head and he nods giving me a kiss on my forehead

"Come on let's go eat something you must be hungry." Azrael says kissing my cheek, ignoring what he was about to ask.

"Hey angel, how'd you sleep?" Ezra asks looking at me concerned

I give him a soft smile "I slept good, thank you. I'm gonna take a shower first than I'll meet you guys downstairs." I tell them, they both nod

I get up walk into the restroom getting some clothes on the way in and turn on the shower.Getting undressed I walk into the shower feeling the hot water hit my skin relaxing my muscles.

Feeing cold air hit me I turn to see Ace getting in naked, his eyes travel down my my body landing on my breast making him smirk.

Looking up he sees I'm watching him and he smiles innocently. Weirdo

"The guys wouldn't stop asking questions so I told them to leave, are you okay?" He asks me again, gently hugging me, I sigh at the comfort his hug brings me

"Yeah I'm okay, besides the soreness I feel, I'm okay. Are you okay?" I ask him putting my chin on his chest to look up at him

"Yes darling i'm okay, I'll bring you some pain killers and food after we shower okay?" he asks looking down at me

"It's okay I'll just walk downstairs, I have to get the exercise. Don't worry." I tell him running my hands through his his hair, I turn around to grab the body wash until-

"Holy fuck!" Ace yells loudly behind me, I turn around quickly and see he's holding his chest that's all red. I try not to laugh

"That's fucking hot Eden, god damn you girls really like hot water during a shower? That shits fucking hot, it's going to melt your skin off damn." He tells me look at me with wide eyes

Finally I burst out and start laughing holding my stomach, I looks through my teary eyes and see Ace smiling down at me.

I turn the hot water down and put turn on cold water a little so it's warm. Taking his hand I drag him under the water and he relaxes. "Finally." He groans throwing his head back

Getting the wash rag I pour some body wash on it and start washing him.

Dragging the cloth down his neck, chest, slowly down his chest until I'm right above his hard on. Barley running my fingers on his tip he quietly groans, his breathing picks up and I just continue washing him making him whine causing me to laugh at him.

After I'm done washing him I take the wash rag and put some body wash on it. As I'm about to scrub myself down Ace stops me.

He grabs the cloth from my hands and starts washing me like I did to him.

⚠️⚠️⚠️

"My turn darling." Is all he says before he continues.

When he reaches my chest area his eyes darkened looking at my breast. Slowly washing my breast he massages them in both hands, squeezing them earning a moan from me. He licks his lips and bring his head down until his lips are the same level as my nipple.

Taking one in his mouth slowly sucking it, he massage's the other. After a minute he switch to the other one giving it the same attention, licking, sucking, biting.

Making me a panting mess.

Letting go of my nipple with a pop he looks at both of them and smirks, looking back at me he says "There you go, both cleaned." Leaning down to kiss me he breaks the kiss

Grabbing the cloth again he starts to wash me again, getting to my legs he painfully drags the cloth up my inner thigh slowly, while keep eye contact with me.

My breathing quickens as he gets closer to where I need him.

Seeing my reaction he smirks and drops the wash cloth, dragging his fingers through my wet folds teasingly making me moan.

"Ace please." I beg

"Come on princess, you can do better than that-" he gets cut off by me wrapping my hand around his dick making him groan.

Rubbing circles on my clit he leans down to kiss me.

I move my hand up and down his dick making him pant into the kiss, he puts his head into my neck and groans.

Moving his fingers faster he slips two fingers in and thrusts both of them in and out of me making me move my hips riding his hand.

I move my hand faster trying to match his tempo, both of us a moaning mess.

"Fuck Eden, just like that baby." He says biting down on my neck

"Ace" I moan making him groan

I put my thumb on his tip and gently press making him groans loudly into my ear."Fuck please Eden, please keep going." He begs looking at me as I slow my movements

"Look who's begging now." I whisper against his lips

Groaning he drops to his knees in front of me grabbing the back of my thighs bringing me closer to him. Grabbing my left leg he puts it over his shoulder and licks my slit making me gasp and grab onto his hair.

Taking my clit into his mouth he sucks making me moan, tightening my hold on his hair causing him to groan.

"Fuck, I'll never get tired of the way you taste la mia bella troia." He groans licking me again making my knees buckle

He gently pushes me against the wall and uses his strength to hold me upright

Sucking my clit he inserts two fingers making me clench around him, he looks up at me through hooded eyes and smirks.

Thrusting the finger in and out of me fast, making me see stars.

Feeling the familiar built up in my lower stomach I clench even harder around his fingers making him mumble "So fucking tight."

Licking my clit faster he picks up his pace moving his fingers faster inside me, feeling my orgasm coming I moan throwing my head back.

"Cum baby, cum for me." He says looking up at me, giving on last hard suck to my clit I come hard.

He removes his fingers quickly and licks all my juices up like a starved man as I cum.

He moans at the taste before giving on last kiss to my clit he gets up to his feet smirking down at me.

Seeing my juices on his mouth and chin I reach up to take his head in my hands and bring him down until his face is right in front of me.

I lick all my juices off his chin and kiss him, he grabs my hips and rocks me into his hip.

Slipping my tongue into his mouth he groans and tightens his grip on my hips. I reach down and pump him again making him break the kiss and moan.

Dropping to my knees in front of him he looks down with hooded eyes and wraps my hair in his hans making a fist before guiding me to his dick.

Seeing the pre cum leak out from his tip it makes my mouth water. Though I don't know how to do this.

Seeing my reaction he says "Lick and suck it like a lollipop baby, just like a lollipop." I nod and grab his dick in my hands and lean in to take him in my mouth.

He moans and gently pushes more of him inside my mouth. I lick along his tip, and along the side of his length. Wrapping my hand around whatever's left that I can't fit in my mouth, I squeeze him making him tighten his grip on my hair.

Feeling him but the back of my throat I'm surprised I didn't gag. I'm proud of myself.

Giving me time to adjust, I start to move my head back and forth, hitting the back of my throat every time. Getting more confident I suck in my cheeks more and move my hand with my mouth, quickening up the pace.

Once I find a rhythm I look up at to see him looking down at me, he throws his head back and releases his lip letting out a loud groan.

Moving his hips, his dick goes further down my throat. Holding breath I take it. All.

I choke but quickly recover, grabbing his balls in my hand I squeeze them making his hips buckle against my hold.

Okay so I learned something about the males body, about a gspot and I want to try it. On him. Let's just hope this goes as planned.

As he continues to thrusting his hips, I take this opportunity to grab his ass in my hands.

Oh, they fat ass fuck!

I move my head to match the rhythm of his thrusts I pull back and take a breath. Lick the his tip, i suck on it making him bite his lips.

"Jesus Eden, you're going to make me cum." He says looking down at me, I smile and reply "Well that's the plan." Causing him to laugh, he chokes when I take him back in my mouth and pump him again with my hand, I occasionally twisting my hand.

With my other hand I slowly drag my hand up until I light brush my finger over that spot, causing him to freeze and look down at me confused.

"Relax, I want to try something." I tell him calmly, he nods.

I stick out my tongue and he gets the idea and puts his dick back into my mouth, my left hand goes to his thigh to steady myself, while the other is still in the same spot.

Slowly moving his hips he moans quietly, brushing my finger over the rim of his hole I gently push my finger inside him making him gasp and shiver at the feeling.

I give his dick a long suck making his hips tremble, moaning and groaning. His breathing goes uneven and he moves his hips more, his dick reaches the back of my throat making my eyes tear up and I don't care.

He moves his dick faster in and out my mouth "Holy fuck Eden, that feels- that feels fucking good. Holy shit." He whimpers while fucking my mouth

Looking up I see his eyebrows drawn together, lips in a 'O' shape no noise is coming out. His head hangs down, taking one long exhale he inhaled and looks at me.

I smirk and curling my finger inside him making him groan loudly, his dick twitches in my mouth, his hips buckle. Sucking him hard I lick his tip and lick the side of his dick.

"Eden, Eden, fuck I'm going to cum." He says

"così fottutamente buono mio dio" He mumbles under breath, with that he cums with a loud moan throwing his head back against the shower wall.

He releases into my mouth, feeling his cum hits the back of my throat. I swallow every single drop, licking him clean.

He goes limp against the shower wall, trying to calm down.

Shaking.

I pull my finger out him and slowly suck him, letting him ride out his orgasm. His dick twitches in my mouth, as he lazily moves his hips back and forth.

Giving one last kiss to his tip he looks at me trying to catch his breath, seeing the sweat on his forehead I get up and kiss him.

⚠️⚠️⚠️

He moans and grips my hips and we rub against each other lazily. Pulling away breathless I lean my forehead against his and smile. "Was that okay?" I ask softly

"'Okay?' Baby that was fucking amazing! Holy fuck I never knew I could feel like that, never have I ever had such a powerful orgasm. That was the best blowjob I've ever gotten, thank you baby." He says looking me in the eyes with adoration, smiling.

"Are you okay? I didn't hurt you did it?" He asks me, I shake my head in return "No you didn't, I needed that thank you. Now I feel much better." I says quietly feeling a blush come up on my cheeks making him laugh.

I smile and give him one last kiss before I grab the wash cloth, put soap on it and clean him again.

Surprisingly the waters still warm.

Eventually we both clean each other and get done with the shower.

•*❀☾❀*•

• *~▫• *~▫• *~▫• *~▫• *~*▫• *~▫• *~▫•Hi.

Sorry I haven't update yet, I ain't graduating as you all know my mental health is shit rn, even mor because of all that's been going on.

My mental health got the best of me and it caused me to lack so much in school so yeah there's that.

Anyways, hope you beautiful horny fucks enjoyed this chapter!

DON'T FORGET TO VOTE, COMMENT, FOLLOW, AND SHARE! <3

STAY SEXY!!

Toodles, I love you!

•. 17 .•

Ace's Pov-

God damn this woman, she literally sucked the living soul out of me, and she walks around innocently?

Call me dramatic, because holy fuck that was the best blowjob I've ever gotten. I've never felt like that, and never have I ever had someone stick their fucking finger in my ass. But I ain't complaining, that felt fucking good.

We walk down the stair hand in hand and see the guys sitting at the table.

"Go ahead and get you food angel, I'll be right there." I give her a kiss on the forehead and turn to see the guys

"Fucking finally, what took you guys so long?" Ezra asks me, looking up from his plate with a curious expression

"We took a shower." I tell them, by the looks they're giving me they don't believe me.

"Only a shower?" Azrael asks me slowly staring into my fucking soul, this guy I swear.

"No...okay...well she gave me blowjob. And holy fuck let me tell right now, that was the best blowjob I've gotten I kid you not. I don't know where she learned, because she literally sucked the fucking soul out of me." I say quietly but quickly said all in one breath

Looking at their wide eyes I give them an innocent smile

"The soul out of you? Are you fucking kidding me, was it that good?" Ezra asks quietly, so Eden won't hear

"Yes it was fucking good, when I say she sucked the living fuck out of me I mean it. She did this thing, but I won't say what because I'll let y'all find out on your own." I tell both of them

"And she's never had experience?" Azrael asks

"No this was her first time, and she made me cum in such short time." I exclaimed

"Well shit-" Ezra says but gets cut off by Eden walking into the dinning room

"Hey guys." She says smiling innocently as if she wasn't just sucking my dick a few minutes ago.

"Hey love, sit down we want to talk to you." Azrael tells Eden, she nods and sits down

I go to get my food and once I do that, I take a seat at the table next to Eden.

"Okay so we wanted to you stay here with us, like live with us you know? Because it's not safe out there, and we want to keep you safe. We'll teach you how to handle a gun again, fight, throw knives, and all that stuff. It's for your own safety. You wouldn't mind living with us idiots right?" Azrael asks looking at Eden intently

"No, I don't want to live here." She says seriously, my heart drops hearing those words. We all looked at her hurt and shocked, but she smiles and bounces in her seat. "I'm kidding I'd love to live here with you guys." She tells us, we all let out a breath of relief and slouch in our chairs

"Don't do that angel." Ezra laughs kissing her head

"I'm sorry, I just wanted to mess with you guys." Giving each of us a kiss on our lips "Let's eat shall we?"

We nod and we go back to eating.

•*❀☽❀*•

•*❀☽❀*•

"No more, no more, I can't keep up." Eden yells dropping to the floor like a sack of potatoes

We've been training for two hours, and over that time she's becoming really good at fighting. She throws me around like a rag doll, and I say thank you.

Anyways her fighting is fucking hot, the sweat on her skin, the look of concentration on her face, it all makes her fucking hot.

"We'll stop for now, because you're tired and have all that exercise today and yesterday. You're a fast leaner so that good, everything you did is good. Good form, good strength, and good job at finding weak spots. I'm proud of you love." I tell her, giving her a good ol sweet kiss on her sweet ass lips, god this woman

"I really love you tattoos." She mumbles against my lips

"Really?" I ask

"Mhm, do they have any meaning?" She asks me, tracing her finger along the lines on my chest. "Yes baby they have meaning, do you want a tattoo?" I ask her

"Yeah I do, I just don't know what to get. There are so many designs to choose, designs to make, I can't choose." She tells me, I hum and kiss her again

"You going to sleep with Ezra tonight?" I ask her, she nods and bites her lip

"Okay well let's go upstairs, oh yeah the guys wanted to ask if you wanted to go to the club with us in a few hours, since we killed all the people who kidnapped you, we still need to be careful. You have to stay with all three of us, or one of us, depending on where you're going. We own this club, so if you want to get away for awhile you can go to our office in there, or we can just go back home. Okay? " I tell her, holding her beautiful hips in my hands

"Oh sounds fun! Do I need to dress up?" She ask innocently. This girl

"Yes baby you have to dress up, anyway you want. Okay?" I laugh lightly telling her, she nods.

I turn around to walk out when I feel two pairs of arms around my waist, lifting me off my feet, Eden throws me backwards with her behind me falling as well. I land on my back making me see stars, holy fuck!

THIS GIRL IS THE FUCKING HULK GOD DAMN!

I groan and slowly sit in a sitting position, hanging my head low I inhale and exhale. I hear laughing and look up to see Eden laughing, while Ezra and Azrael stand there in complete shock.

"Oh baby I'm sorry, I just wanted to see if I could do while you were distracted." She tells me wrapping her arm around my waist kissing me.

I grip her ass in my hands and squeeze kissing her back. She grinds herself against me, making me go hard at the little friction. I slowly put my thigh between her legs, gripping her ass I rock her against my thigh making her moan.

I hear groans a second later, I look to see who it is only to see Azrael and Ezra rubbing themselves through their pants seeing they go hard.

She hear them and breaks the kiss, looking back she seeing them rubbing their hard on. Through hooded eyes she looking at their hands, she bits her lips and her breathing quickens.

My baby likes watching and being watched.

She breaks away from my hold making me pout, but she kisses me and walks away.

Going towards both of them she touches their chests slowly dragging her fingers down their chest. Not breaking eyes contact with them smirking she palms both of them, making them gasp and thrust their hips forward into her hand more.

I groan rubbing myself through my pants, feeling what they're feeling right now as she touches them.

Gently kneading both of their dicks in her hands she goes on her toes and kisses them both. They groan into the kiss and gripping her hips lightly.

Ezra sucks on her neck, while Azrael kisses her hard. Breaking the kiss, Ezra back away from her neck and looks down at her.

Leaning between both of them, she whispers in their ears "Sorry boys, but I have to go change."

Letting go of their jean-clad dicks they groan in frustration and fall onto the mat, she smirks down at them winking before she turns to leave. Blowing a kiss at all three of us before walking out the door.

Leaving all three of us extremely hard well I guess it a cold shower today.

This woman is killing us.

•*❀☽❀*•

• *~▫• *~▫• *~▫• *~▫• *~*▫• *~▫• *~▫•Hi.

I don't know what you say anymore.

Toodles, I love you! <3

•. 18 .•

Third Person Pov-

It's been two hours since Ace and Eden got done training, they all showered in cold water, get ready and met up in the living room to wait. Now the guys are all sitting in the living room waiting for Eden, who's still getting ready.

She can take as long as she wants, they don't mind waiting on her.

"You think she's okay with going to the club?" Ezra says breaking the silence, both Ace and Azrael look up from their phones thinking about what Ezra asked them.

"She's 19, but I'm sure she's okay with going there. Besides she needs to explore more and do new things. So I think she'll be fine, as long as she stays by us." Azrael says rubbing his chin, all he can think about is her getting kidnapped again making him nauseous.

"Did you find out who's behind the kidnapping?" Ace asks while getting more comfortable on the chair he's sitting on

"No me and the team are still working on it, it looks like most of the guys that we killed were just their men. Because none of them are in charge, Leo wasn't in charge. He just volunteered and shit. So we don't know who's really behind the kidnapping." Ezra tells both Ace and Azrael who are thinking about his words, they nod and just hope it doesn't happen again.

Hearing the click of heels coming towards them, they all look to see and they immediately freeze in their spots.

Eyes wide open, mouth slightly agape, all their focus was on Eden who looked stunning.

Immediately their dicks all harden at the sight of her, making them shift on their feet feeling their pants get small.

'Holy shit' was all they can think at the moment.

Eden looks at them wondering whats wrong with them, should she get them water? Food? They look at her with wide eyes making her think that the dress she choose was to revealing.

'Should I change?' was what she thought, while looking at the three beautiful men in front of her. •*❀☽❀*•

•*❀☽❀*•Eden's Pov-

Making my way down the hallway to the living room my heels making noise with every step I took, making me feel powerful.

Walking into the living room I see their eyes go wide and mouth open, just like when they took me on our first date. I smile at the memory.

After about a minute, they're still staring at me.

'Is my dress to short?''Do they not like it?''Should I change?''I feel hot, I hope they don't make me change.'

All these thoughts are going through my head, I didn't even notice they're all standing in front of me with a look of lust in their eyes.

"Should I change? Is this too much?" They know I struggle with my image and how I see myself they immediately shake their heads and smile at me

"You look gorgeous baby." Azrael tells me

Seeing their tattoos on display, makes my core ache with need.

"You guys look hot." I blurt out, making my eyes go wide at the statement I just made

They all step forward and lean down, Ace going behind me putting his head in neck. Azrael standing in front of me,with his hand on my cheek, and Ezra who's at my side drawing featherlight hearts on my breasts making my breathing quicken quietly.

Looking into Azraels eyes I look down at his lips and back up. Getting the message he leans down and kisses me, taking my bottom lip between his teeth. I lightly moan at the feeling.

He back away from my touch so Ace and Ezra can kiss me too.

"You look stunning Angel." Ezra mumbles against my lips, I smile and say "You too baby." Kissing me one last time Ace pushes him out the way making him trip and fall.

I laugh at them and turn back to Ace who's looking at me with lust and adoration. "My beautiful Eden, I can't stop looking at you." He tells me, kissing me he slips his tongue into my mouth and groans when I do the same.

After a minute I pull away and while the corner of his mouth. Looking at Azrael and Ezra they both look at us with a heated gaze making me feel naked-

"Well let's go." I say and happily hop to the door and to the car

•*❀ ☽ ❀*•

•*❀ ☽ ❀*•

We made it to the club, and there's a lot of people here grinding non each other, making out, or people just staring at us.

Guys looking at me with list in their eyes, girls looking at me jealous.

"Come on baby, let's go find a booth." Azrael says to me putting a hand around my waist, guiding us through the sweat bodies.

"Here sit right here love, do you want anything to drink?" Azrael asks me

"Hm-what? I can drink?" I ask confused yet surprised, they all nod "Only on drink though, we don't want you to have a hang over." Ace says tucking a piece of hair behind my ear

"Okay than can I get a Cherry Lime Tequila Cocktail please? Thank you." I tell them, Ezra gets up from the booth "I'm gonna go get the drinks, guy you want the usual?" Ezra asks them, they nod and he goes to the bar to order

"You okay?" Ace asks me, putting a hand on my thigh, I nod and lean my head on his shoulder, he kisses the rope of my head

"Mhm, yup peachy! Do you know where the bathroom is?" I didn't go to the restroom yet since training, at the time I didn't need to go, but right now I really do.

"You okay going alone? Or do you want me to go with you?" Ace asks me, looking unsure

"It's okay I'll go by myself." I tell him, he nods and gives me directions "Go down this hallway take a right, and it's the first door on the right side, "be careful love." Azrael says, giving me a kiss on my lips, I nod and get up from the booth

Feeling someone eyes on me I keep going.

5 minutes later

I'm washing my hands and the soap smells really good. The door opens and a woman walks in, she looks at me through the mirror.

"Hi I'm Chloe, and I want to ask if those guys were Ace, Ezra, and what's his name again? Oh yes Azrael." She says their names seductively making me cringe

"Yeah those are their name." I say quietly

"Are you fucking them?" She asks making me choke on fucking air"I can't answer that sorry." I tell her looking at her, she sees me looking and smirks at me.

"Too bad, they're a good fuck." She tells me, touching up her lipgloss

"What?" I ask confused

"I said they're a good fuck, mine personally was fucking good. Ugh, especially Azrael my god. He can fuck for hours on end, Ace can make you feel like you're floating. And Ezra well, he's good at eating pussy I'll tell you that." She tells me, I stand there shocked

"God do I miss their dicks, they were so rough in the sheets. Always told me how beautiful I was, give me kisses on the cheeks and lips.

Tell me I'm all theirs. But they just dumped me like I was trash." She says running her fingers through her hair

"I'm a 10 and what are you? 2?" She laughs at me making me feel uncomfortable "Come-on I mean in a room full of hot girls who do you think they'll pick? Huh? Think about it, if you and hundreds of other woman were in the same room, do you honestly think they'll choose you?" She asks looking at me with disgust and hate

"They can find someone more curvy and hot. But they had to choose you? My god give me strength, it hurts just by looking at you. You dress like a slut, look at you, showing your fucking cleavage and all that stuff. You're just being a desperate whore." She tells me, making me feel disgusted in my own skin. I take a step back and hold myself up against the wall behind me.

"Like I said a good fuck, they'll just use you like the trash you are and leave your pathetic ugly ass." With that she walks out leaving me to feel ugly in my own skin, I look in the mirror and see myself

I don't like what I see

I think that over, and over, and over. Feeling tears prick my eyes I inhale and exhale over and over again.

I stop the voice recorder, because I want to show one of them what she said to me.

After I've done that, I feel rage. She didn't have to destroy my self confidence, fucking bitch. I'm worth more than her, and she told me all this because of some jealousy she's feeling? Bitch

But she didn't have to go that hard.

•*❀ ☽ ❀*•

• *~▫• *~▫• *~▫• *~▫• *~*▫• *~▫• *~▫•Hi.

I don't know- vote I guess?

Toodles, I love you!

•. 19 .•

Ezra's Pov-

Setting the drinks down on the table, I see that Eden's not here. I start to panic but Ace is quick to say "She went to the restroom, she'll be back." At that I immediately calm down

"How long has she been in there?" His eyebrows furrowed as he looked at his watch "About 10 minutes, the fuck." I nod and stand up from the booth

"I'm going to go check on her, see if she's okay." I tell them, they both nod and I make my way to the girls bathroom

As I near the door, I hear someone sniffing. I knock on the door and I hear a faint 'come in'. Why's my baby crying?

I open the door and the first thing I see is Eden sitting on floor with her head in her arms.

Turning around to lock the door and kneel in front of her. "Hey angel why are you crying?" I ask softly, trying not to scare her. She hands me her phone and my eyebrows furrowed looking at it.

What am I supposed to do with this?

She takes it back and opens the phone, pulling up a voice recording. Okay now I'm even more confused. She hands it back to me and I press play.

After a few minutes of listening to the recording, my blood boiled. This bitch really thought it's okay to say she slept with us and say we're using her for her fucking body, when we've never met her before. Even worse she made my girl cry, and destroyed her self confidence. She was barley starting to feel comfortable in her own skin. My poor baby.

"Hey baby don't listen to her, we've never slept with her. I don't recognize her voice or her name, I'd choose you over any girl in a room full of them. I'll always choose you Eden. Don't listen to her, you're beautiful inside and out. She's just jealous because you're with us, and I'm sorry she said those things to you. You're nothing she said you were, because we know you. she don't. Don't put your self down over what she said because you my beautiful, hot, gorgeous angel. No one compares to you. No one." I tell her softly, seeing more tears fall down her face I kiss them, her eyes, nose, forehead, both cheeks, and finally her lips.

"Your beautiful Eden." I say hugging her, I double tap her thighs and she wraps them around my waist. Clinging to me as if I'll disappear. I walk both of us around back and forward in the bathroom trying to calm her down. Maybe me too, because what she said about us using her like a fucking piece of meat was the last fucking straw.

Kissing her head I rock both of us side to side."You're okay now angel, I'm here. You're okay." I whisper to her, laying my head on hers. Letting her calm down.

•*❀☽❀*•

•*❀☽❀*•

Alright I think it's been long enough.

I give her one last kiss before I take her back out, and to the booth. Music blasting through the speakers, people talking and dancing all over the place. But lucky our booth is in the corner away from the noise and people.

They see me carrying Eden and they immediately walk over to us both looking worried. "Eden darling what happened?" Ace asks her lightly, running his finger through her hair

Her head on my shoulder she looks at Ace, but doesn't say anything. Seeing her bottom lip wobble she turns her head burying her face into my neck.

"Eden what happened? What's wrong?" Azrael asks getting more worried about her trying to gently take her from my arms but she tightens her grip on me

"It's okay Eden, go to sleep for awhile baby. I'll talk to them." I whisper into her ear, rubbing her back softly

"Let go to the office." I tell them, they both nod and we make our way to the office upstairs

Once we get up there, I feel that Eden's breathing had even out telling me she's sleeping. Taking her the bed in the other room of the office, I set her down gently and pull a blanket over her, kissing her head I make my way to the guys in the other room. Closing the door gently behind me.

We usually sleep here if we have work, or are just tired sometimes.

The office is a no sex zone, so we just stay here by ourselves sometimes to work, or if it's late.

"What happened to her? And why was she crying?" Ace immediately asks me as soon as I walk into the room

"She's sleeping now, I think all the crying got her tired. This was supposed to be a fun night for her. But someone had to ruin it." I sigh and take a seat in one of the two chairs in front of the desk, looking at both of them I take out Eden's phone, unlock it, and pull up the voice recording pressing play for them to listen.

After the recording is over the guys are furious.

"Who the fuck is Chloe?" Azrael asks looking at both of us "I would ask the same because I have no fucking clue who this bitch is." Ace tells him

"That's why Eden was crying because of what she told her. She probably believes we're going to do that to her, just up and leave. The fucking bitch called her a slut, and made her cry. We never even fucking slept with a bitch named Chloe." I say angrily leaning back further into the chair

"I don't like what she said, about us, and about Eden. Not one bit." Ace tells both of us

"Let's go find her." Azrael says dangerously calm, making me slightly shiver. This Azrael is creepy as fuck.

"Yeah let's do it." I say, they both nod in agreement. We stand up and make our way out quietly not to wake her up

We make it down stairs, met with the smell of alcohol, music blasting, people talking.And drunk people swaying all over the place.

"Alright let's go find this Chloe girl." Azrael says to both of us, we nod in reply "Let's go separate ways, and see if we can find her." I say, I walk to the back of the club, Azrael goes to the dance floor, while Ace goes to the bar

Feeling someone arms around my waist, I look back and see a blond haired girl, with fake ass tits and ass. Her lip have fillers in it, seeing she put on- what's that? Contacts?

"Hey handsome you're Ezra right?" That voice, the same voice from the recording.

It's her

"Hey baby, you want to go to the back room with us?" I lied, there's no back rooms.

Running her fingers down my chest, she tries to bat her lashes at me. But I try not to throw up all over this bitch.

"Yeah sure let's go, you can bring your friends if you'd like, I love to party." She tries to purr, but miserably fails, I just want to go back to Eden. But I'm to busy trying not to kill this bitch

"Whatever you want baby." I try not to cringe at what I'm saying to her, seeing she's satisfied we walk towards Ace who's sitting at the bar looking around. Tapping on his shoulder he turns and looks at me before looking at the girl next to me. Raising his eyebrow at me I wink at him, and he gets up smirking at her.

"Hey doll what's your name?" He asks her leaning against the counter

"My names Chloe sugar." She tells him and he looks at me in surprise before it turns to a glare, Azrael comes over and sees what's happening, he glared at the girl but she doesn't notice.

She's too busy trying to show her fake tits to Ace who's looking at Azrael.

He nods and we make our way to the door in back, I wrap someone random tie around her eyes so she won't see where we're going, and lead her to the basement.

"Where are we going?" She laughs trying to feel where we're going, walking down the stairs we stop once we get to the door.

Unlocking it, we sit her down in the metal chair making her grin drop and she shivers at the cold feeling of the chair.

"Uh guys? What are you doing?" She asks nervously making me smirk

"The her to the chair." Azrael says and we immediately do that.

"Let go, no please. Let me go I didn't do anything wrong!" She yells at us trying to pull at the ropes around her ankles and wrist

"Play it." Ace says, I pull out the phone and play it. Ignoring the girl's questions.

Hearing the audio playing she pales.

"You made our girl cry. Why?" Azrael asks dangerously clam. Yeeeeee

"I-I don't know...I just...She..." she stutters making us smirk

"Oh what you can't talk now? You made her cry, and you said that we slept with you, we don't even know who the fuck you are. You should've kept your fucking mouth shut. And now you'll pay for everything you said and done to her. She had was slowly getting confident, you had to show up and ruin that for her. " Ace tells her, making her shake

"Let's go, we'll let Eden have some fun with her when she's up." Azrael tells us looking at her smirk, we nod and make our way to the door, turning off the lights leaving her in the dark.

We make up back up before she's awake, walking into the bedroom we see her laying down holding a pillow. Aw

"Let's get her into something different, I don't want her to be uncomfortable sleeping." Ace says, we nod and walk over to her

I start taking off her dress, slowly not to wake her up. Ace takes off her heels, while Azrael gently wipes off her makeup.

Bringing the straps off her shoulders I gently tug it down but stop when her breast are about to show. Fuck she's not wearing a bra.Walking over to the walk in closet, I get a black shirt and go back into the room seeing Azrael and Ace watching her.

I pull it over head, while Azrael and Ace put her arms through the shirt. Seeing they did it, I pull the shirt down to her waist so it's on her, when it's on her I reach under the shirt and grab the dress ends around her chest area and gently pull it down.

The shirt covers her chest, though we've already seen her breast. We still want her to show us when she wants to, we'll not look unless she shows us, other than that we won't look. Especially since she's sleeping.

I drag the dress off her from under the shirt and finally take it off her. Putting it on the chair beside the bed I see her heels right there to.

I kiss her forehead and go to the bathroom to brush my teeth. Ace comes in and brushes his teeth as well.

"I'm gonna go to the office and tell everyone it's closing time, I'll be back." Azrael says walking out the room

Taking off my shirt and pants, Ace does the same and we move to lay next to her.

I sigh and lay down next to Eden, putting my face into her neck softly kissing her necklace. I love laying next to her.

Ace goes to the other side of her and lays down putting his head on her shoulder, kissing it he starts closing his eyes. Feeling hands run through my hair I see it's Edens hands, both her hands in me and Aces hair gently going through it. We smile and slowly start to go to sleep.

A few minutes later Azrael comes into the room removing his shirt and pants. He lays down between Eden's legs and puts his head on her stomach. Wrapping his arms around her waist.

Eden let's go of me and Aces hair making me pout. She runs both her fingers through Azraels hair , he sighs and kisses her stomach.

Finally sleep consumes us all.

•*❦☽❦*•

• *~▫• *~▫• *~▫• *~▫• *~*▫• *~▫• *~▫•Hi.

I went to my cousins school to see him graduate, and I ran into the people that used to bully me in school. And they just stared at me, we didn't know what to do. Next thing you know, I needed my inhaler. A bitch was having a panic attack.

I don't know- vote I guess?

Toodles, I love you!

•. 20 .•

Eden's Pov-

I open my eyes and see I'm not in any of the rooms at home. Where am I?

Looking around I see Ezra's head tucked into my neck, holding onto my arm like I'm going to disappear. Looking to my other side I see Aces head on my shoulder, him lightly snoring with a pout. Cute.

Looking down I see Azraels head under my shirt, hm someone changed me. His face is in my boobs, and I'm not wearing any bra. Peachy.

"Dude get your head out my boobs." I whisper yelling at him quietly not to wake the other two

He starts steering, and finally looks up smirking at me. "No I love them, leave me alone." He tells me, giving both my nipple a light kiss making me moan quietly

I need to go to the restroom, and shower.

I start to get up, when all they put more of their weight on me while groaning, making me sigh.

"I need to go shower." I tell them, they all groan and mumble 'no' in their morning voices making me heat up. Jesus

"Shut up go back to sleep." Ace says in his morning voice

I huff in annoyance and give up, they smile giving me an a small kiss going back to sleep.

It's been like 5 minutes all I've been thinking about was what happened last night. That girl, make me feel so many things. But Ezra fixed it, fixed me, and what he told me I trusted him. A few seconds go by and I try again. "I have to take a shower." I tell them, they all groan but move off me. Making me smile and stretch, they all lay back on the bed going to sleep.

I get off the bed and see them all laying there, eyes still closed.

I don't know if I should ask, should I?Oh fuck it, you only live once.

"Wanna shower with me?" I ask them, they immediately open their eyes and sit up looking at me with wide eyes to see if I really asked that.

"What did you say?" Ezra asks

"I asked if you guys want to take a shower with me. Unless you guys don't want to, it's fine if you don't want to." I told them

'No we want to."Let's go take a shower than."No,no,no,no'

They all say at the same time, making me smile. I walk through the door taking off my shirt, showing my black lacy underwear, and my breast. Turning around they're all standing there looking at me, Ace looking at my ass, Ezra biting his lip looking at my breast, and Azrael who's eyeing me up and down with a smirk.

I may not be all that confident in myself, but when they stare at me it all goes away. Their gaze makes me feel hot and confident.

Yeah that girl made me feel like shit, but she just gave me more strength in myself. When people hate on you, they're jealous. What they say to you, only makes you stronger.

These three men in front of me, make me feel so much. I let them see my body because I know they won't judge me, I trust them with my body.

I slowly tease them, by taking off my underwear. Sliding it down my legs, my back turned towards them.

"Fuck" I hear Ezra whisper looking at my naked body

Looking down I see all of them hard, I smirk walking over to them palming Ace and Ezra making them push their hips further into my hand. I gently squeeze making them groan and I let go causing them to let if a frustrated groan. Going over to Ezra I run both my hands down his chest, until my fingers are on his boxers. Tugging them down slowly, he groans looking at me in the eyes. Pulling the boxers forward I let go, making it lightly smack his stomach.

"Fucking tease." Ace says running his hard on, the other two doing the same.

I walk away from them smirking and get in the shower, once I'm in I look through the glass seeing them take off their boxers and coming in.

Ace on the other hand almost fell trying to get off his boxers quickly, making me laugh at him.

"How'd you sleep my love?" Azrael asks wrapping his arms around me, hugging me to him.

I lean into his touch and sigh "I slept like a baby. And you?" I ask grabbing the loofah with body wash, poring some on and start to wash him

"I slept really great, best sleep I've had." He tells me "You're only saying that because you slept on my boobs." I say making him smirk

Ace and Ezra come over and kiss me on the cheeks, they grab my ass and knead both in their hands making me lightly moan. "Let's get you cleaned up, shall we?" Ace whispers in my ear, gently biting it

I nod and they start to wash me, I swear they make my heart go crazy. These men will be the death of me.

•*❀☽❀*•

•*❀☽❀*•

After the shower we brush our teeth as I'm about to walk out the bathroom, someone grabs my waist turning me around to face them.

Seeing it's Ezra he leans in and kisses me hard, his tongue brushing against mine making me moan tugging onto his hair.

Feeling another pair of arms around my waist I feel kisses on my neck.

I let go of Ezra and turn to see Ace standing their, I grab his shirt and tug him to me. His lips landing on mine, in a passionate kiss. His kisses are always soft and passionate.

Giving him and Ezra one last kiss I walk to Azrael who's watching intently, he sees me coming and straightens his posture. I run my hands over both his cheeks making him close his eyes, gently bringing him down I kiss him.

He immediately responds grabbing my hips pulling me closer to him. He bites my lip and licks it, his tongue slides into my mouth, I gasp when his hands squeeze my ass making me moan at the feeling. He smiles and gives me one last kiss before letting go.

I kiss their foreheads and walk into the room, sitting on the bed waiting for them.

"We've got a surprise for you Angel." Ezra tells me, I start to bounce in my seat

"Oh surprise? Yay! What is it now? Another person? Male or Female?" I ask making them chuckle

"You'll see, I'd say this is payback." Ace whispers to me

We walk down the stairs and into the basement, hm kinda creepy but okay. Going to the first door Azrael unlocks it and it's dark inside, hearing a woman crying I turn on the lights only to be met with that bitch again.

"Help me, please help me. They took me down here last night, I don't why please help me." Chloe pleads looking at me desperately

"I don't want to see her face any longer, can we hurry this up?" I ask them, and they nod understandingly

Walking over to the weapon table ignoring her pleading I see a gun, 'now's the perfect time to do some target practice' I tell myself, picking up the beautiful baby, I walk over to her and hold the gun to her.

Her eyes go wide, face drains of all colors. I smile at her and shoot her left shoulder, right shoulder, both hands, both knee caps, both feet, she screams none stop so I slap her.

"Shut the fuck up, god you're annoying." I tell her "See you in hell." pulling the trigger, the bullet going between her eyes, her eyes go wide and mouth opens, finally the life drains of her eyes and she goes limp in her chair making me smile.

Turning around I see the guys looking at me with proud eyes.

"Eden I swear we never slept with her, we've never seen her until last night. You're absolutely beautiful the way you are okay baby? You're perfect." Azrael tells me hugging me, giving my head a kiss.

"Okay, I believe you." I whisper into his chest

I let go and Ace pulls me into a hug lifting me off my feet, making me laugh.

"Eden darling, I like you so fucking much it hurts. So listen to me when I say, you're the only woman I'll ever feel this way about. No one can live up to your perfection, no one. You're beautiful you're own ways, and I will always like you for you. You're nothing she said you were, because we know who you are. You're my beautiful and gorgeous girl, no one will ever hurt you." He whispers into my ear, feeling tears prick the corner of my eyes I don't let them fall. These men mean so much to me, I can't explain it.

"We'll always like you, and only you no matter what. You our hearts, souls, and body." He adds on, I kiss him deeply and tug his hair trying to get more feel of him.

I let go and smile at all of them.

"I trust you guys with my body and soul, you guys have my trust. And I will always trust you guys, no matter what anyone says." I tell smiling at them softly, they return it ten times bigger.

"Can we eat something, and I'm still kind of tired can we go home? I want to take a nap." I say, rubbing my tummy before patting it

They smile and kiss me, we make our way to the car and get in.

Home here we come.

•*❀☽❀*•

• *~☐• *~☐• *~☐• *~☐• *~*☐• *~☐• *~☐•

Hi.

Bye.

•. 21 .•

 Warning this chapter is a bit Steamy in it x

Edens Pov-

"I'm still kind of tired I'm going to go take a nap upstairs." I tell them, they all nod as I'm about to go upstairs I get stopped.

"Who's room are you sleeping in?" Azrael asks, ugh he's got a point

"Ezra's room, if that's okay with him." I reply "Yes that's okay Angel, you can sleep in my room anytime you want. I'll up in a bit okay?" He tells me, I nod give him a kiss on his cheek and walk upstairs

Walking into Ezra's room I take off my pants leaving me in white lacy underwear, and take off my bra because that shits to uncomfortable to sleep in.

I lay down on his bed, getting comfortable. His bed is so soft, I sigh getting under the covers, and lay on my side.

Closing my eyes I let sleep take over me.

•*❀ ☽ ❀*•

The bed moving wakes me up, I turn and see Ezra getting into bed behind me, he has no shirt on or pants, only his boxers, hot. I smile lazily at him to which he returns "I'm sorry angel I didn't mean to wake you, go back to sleep." He whispers to me, I hum and go back to sleep, with him behind me.

Feeling his arm wrap itself around my waist pulling me back until my back is to his chest. I fall asleep with the sound of his breathing

•*❀☽❀*• ⚠⚠⚠

"Eden, stop." Ezra's deep voice wakes me up from my sleep. I don't know what he's talking about, he grabs my hips to stop me from grinding on his dick. Oh

Oops I didn't know I was doing that, what a dream!

His hard dick is pressing against my ass making me want to grind on him more. I must've been grinding myself against him in my sleep. I just stop all movement like he said, and didn't move my hips.

But the feeling of needing him doesn't go away.

This time I move closer to him to finding a bit of friction against his dick. His fingers tighten against my hip, but he doesn't stop me, he wants this as much as me.

"Watch yourself, angel." His mouth is close to my neck, I move my neck to the side to give my space to kiss me. And he does, leaving wet kisses all over my neck. Finding my sweet spot, he starts to suck, making me moan.

I start grinding my ass against him, only this time a little more harder.

A low, rumbling groan fall from his lips and vibrants through my whole body. His hand on my hip control the movements of my grinding, urging me to go on. He pushes his cock against my ass slowly grinding against me.

I moan and put my hand on his at my hips.

Fuck I'm wet, I take his hand and slowly drag it down to my lower stomach, over my underwear, and back up. Finally taking his hand I drag it between my legs showing him how wet I am. The feeling of his hand there creates sparks all over my body.

Once he feels how wet I am, he groans and grinds himself against me much harder. Both our breathing going faster, and faster. Trying to find a friction, to let us both release.

His starts to kiss my neck again, sometimes biting, or sucking. One last bite to my neck he takes his hand out my underwear before taking hold of my underwear and slowly drags it down my legs, leaving me only in a shirt.

Next he takes his boxers are off, leaving him completely naked, grabbing my leg, he drapes it over his so my legs are apart.

His hand returns between my legs, slowly teasing me. Rubbing my clit in slow movements he plunges one thick finger inside me making me moan arching my back.

Thrusting his finger inside me slowly, I grind against his hand trying to rub my clit against the palm of his hand. As if hearing me, he takes his finger out and runs it up and down my slit, before making contact with my clit, causing me to moan.

"So wet piccola puttana sporca." He whispers against my ear, biting it softly. I moan in return, he turns around getting something out the side drawer, seeing it's a condom he opens it with his teeth and roles it onto his dick.

Just seeing it makes me ache for him more.

Moving back behind me, he takes my leg and puts it on top of his. Feeling his cock at my entrance, I move back closer to him. Wanting to be filled by him already.

"Such a needy whore, desperate for dick." He says biting my shoulder "Only for you three." I whisper to him, he groans and takes my leg opening me more for him

His finger still wet with my arousal, holding my hips. Taking his dick in the other hand he bring it to where I need him more he slowly pushes inside me.

We both groan at feeling, after a few second he lets me adjust. I nod for him to go on, slowly pulling out, he thrusts back in, doing that for a more seconds.

"Faster Ezra." I tell him, he groans tightening his hold on my hips before thrusting faster into me.

Bringing his hand between my legs he plays with my clit, I moan arching my back trying to catch my breath.

"Such a good girl." He tells me thrusting faster and harder, I move back making his thrust until he's balls deep inside me.

His finger lace with mine, he brings me even more closer to him. His breathing picks up, trying to catch his breath. Taking my hand he brings it down to my aching clit, and we play with it at the same time.

"H-holy fuck". I whisper breathlessly

The room being filled with the sounds our skin slapping, our moans, and our hard breathing.

Feeling myself get close, I squeeze around him making him moan. "Fuck don't do that or else this will be over really soon." He tells me, both of us grind against each other searching for a release.

"Fuck you feel so good, la mia piccola puttana sporca." He says biting down my shoulder, that feels good

"You feel good." I tell him, he moans around me and pick up his pace.

Feeling his dick twitch inside me I feel that he's close as well.

"Fuck, fuck, fuck, fuck." I say gripping his hand tightly in mine, the build up in my lower stomach coming fast.I squeeze around him again causing him to groan.

"You about to cum? Cum for me baby. Cum over my cock." He says breathlessly, playing my clit again, making me see stars.

With a few more thrust I cum on dick hard, moaning at the feeling I get lost in the euphoric feeling. My body lost in pleasure, as he holds me tightly, his fingers on my clit making my body jerk.

"Sensitive, to sensitive." I tell him, pulling his hand away from my clit, locking our fingers to together. He start thrusting harder inside me, chasing for his release, after a few more thrust he cums with a moan.

We lazily grind against each other, riding out our orgasms together.

We stop or movements, he turns me around and kisses me. The kiss becoming heated real quickly, I pull away and see the sweat on his skin, moving the damp hair away from his eyes, I kiss his forehead.

Pulling away I look at him, only to see he's looking at me with hooded eyes, and adoration.

Giving one last kiss to my lips, he slowly pulls out of me making me hiss at the feeling. He discharge's the condom, tying it up and throw it away into the trash can.

Bye kids!

⚠️⚠️⚠️

He picks me up, and takes me to the restroom running a bath. He goes back into the room to change the sheets, and comes back to get inside to tub with me.

I wash him, and he washes me. Occasionally kissing my lips, shoulders, or massaging my breast making me moan quietly leaning into his touch.

"I love your body angel, you're so fucking beautiful." He whispers into my ear, feeling my eyes well up with tears I turn to him straddling him, I kiss him.

"And you're gorgeous Ezra, perfect all over." I whisper against his lips, feeling his hard dick poke my stomach. I turn and lay down with my back to his chest, his arms wrap themselves around my waist holding me there.

What a day!

•*❀☽❀*•

• *~◻• *~◻• *~◻• *~◻• *~*◻• *~◻• *~◻•Hi.

Thank you for 2.43k reads! I love you.

Bye.

•. 22 .•

Eden's Pov-

We're all eating right now, it's just now 3, me and Ezra slept until 2:30.

And I'm thinking about getting birth control, like the IUD one, because I don't trust the pills. I've heard you can still get pregnant when you're on the pill. And I don't want that, I'm still young, so yeah.

"Can I go to the hospital after we're done eating?" I ask them, they all choke on their food eyes wide, grabbing their drinks before chugging it down.

"What-" Azrael gets cut off when he chokes again

'Are you okay?''What's wrong?''Anything hurt?''Oh my god did we hurt you?''Why do you want to go to the hospital?'

They all ask at the same time, making me smile a bit.

"No, no you guys didn't hurt me or anything. I was just...I just wanted to get a check up, because I wanted to look into something." I tell them slowly getting nervous

"Why do you want to go to the hospital?" Azrael demands looking at me curiously

"Like I said I want to look into something." I tell them, they all look at me concerned, confused, and sternly.

They want to ask more, but they don't which I'm glad they didn't. Nodding their heads hesitantly, I smile and go back to eating.

"Are you sure you're okay? You've got me worried here." Ezra whispers into my ear, I give him a small smile and kiss his cheek, "I'm sure I'm okay, just trust me okay?" I tel him, he nods and goes back to eating

•*❀☾❀*•

•*❀☾❀*•

"Baby are you sure you're okay?" Ace asks me once we pull up to the hospital. I turn from where I'm sitting to look back at him, "For the thousandth time Ace yes I'm okay, don't worry." I tell him, he nods and sighs

"We'll let's go." I say opening the passenger door. Azrael gets out the driver seat, Ace opens his door, and Azrael locks all the doors before Ezra can get out. So Ezra decides to get out the same door as Ace, but Ace closes the door on him before he can get out.

"Ace you fucking bitch! Fuck you!" Ezra yells from inside the car, we all laugh at him, Azrael unlocks the doors making Ace pull open the door causing Ezra to fall out.

Landing on his hands, while his other half of his body is inside the cars still.

We all laugh at him, he gets up dusting himself off. Looking at us he glares, but when his eyes land on me and he pouts. I sigh and walk over to him hugging him "I'm sorry for laughing, I couldn't help it." I chuckle into his chest

He kisses my head "It's okay, as long as you're smiling and laughing than it's all good." He tells me

We make our way to the entrance, going straight to Women's health. They all walk inside the waiting room with me, while I fill out the forms they gave me. Looking them I see they're all nervous, and looking around.

10 minutes later

"Eden Lilith!" The nurse yells, the guys all look at me with big pleading eyes. 'I'll be back.' I mouth to them

We go to the room and I wait for the doctor to come inside.

After a few more boring minutes, the doctor finally walks in. "Hi Eden I'm Dr.Peters and I'll be your doctor today. So tell me Eden what are you in for?" She asks me, looking up from her clipboard

"I'm here for an IUD." I tell her, she and starts asking me questions about my health, "Okay I'll be back with the stuff, and we'll get started. In the mean time I'll need you get under dress, just only your pants and underwear that's all. Once you're done with that, you can put on that gown right there and sit on the table." She says all cheerfully

5 minutes later the doctor finally returns with the supplies she needs and tells me to lay down on the table, putting my feet in some weird holding thing.

She does here thing down there and she says "Alright Eden you did a good job so far, now this time I'll need you to relax, because you'll feel a little pinch. Alright honey? Just breathe." She tells me

I let out a small yell, trying to get away from the pain. Feeling tears fall down my cheeks I try to calm down, but the pains to much.

"Breathe for me Eden, it's almost over." She try's to assure me, after a few seconds she backs away telling me to put my legs down now.

Once I do, I feel a little discomfort down there.

Fuck that hurt like a bitch, still feeling tears fall down my face I wipe them. Taking a deep breath I try to calm down.

"You okay honey?" Dr.Peters asks me, I only nod in return

"Okay for the next 48 hours you can't have sex, and if you're on your period you'll have to use a pad, you should be good in two days." She says

"Alright thank you." I tell her, she smiles at me and write something down "Okay well it was nice meeting you Eden, you can get dressed now, and walk yourself out once you're done. You still remember the way, right?" I nod and smile at her, thanking her she walks out and I get dressed.

Walking into the waiting room I see three girls trying to talk to them, feeling a bit of jealousy I make my way over to them, as I'm about to say something, they see me and jump front their seats bringing me into a tight hug.

"You okay love?" Azrael asks me kissing my lips, looking at me with concern seeing the dry tears on my cheeks

"Yes I'm okay, don't worry. Can we go now?" I ask them softly, their worried gaze turning soft they nod and we all make our way out. Ezra holds my hand while Ace holds the other. Azrael walking ahead of us, just glaring at all the people who looking our way.

They make me feel safe.

Getting into the car I sit down, but don't really feel that discomfort I felt when I got up from my seat in the hospital.

I sigh and lean into my seat.

"Can we get a milkshake?" I ask them, "Sure love, what kind do you want?" Azrael asks starting the car, he puts one hand on my thigh and the other on the steering wheel.

"Mm a strawberry shake." I tell him, he smiles and nods his head looking back at the road

Rubbing circles on my inner thigh his hand going higher and higher, but I put my hand on his stopping him. He looks at me worried, but keeps his hand where it is, not moving it.

We get to the dinner, and make our way inside taking a seat at a booth.

'Oh my god, they're so hot.' Two girls whisper to each other one booth away from us

'Yeah you should get their numbers, see if we can have a little fun with them. I wonder if they're single.' The other girl tell her

Getting up their seats they walk over to our booth and lean on the table, showing their boobs. "Hey hottie's, can I get your numbers?

Maybe we all can have fun together sometimes." The blonde says leaning against Ace, but he only looks at the table not even sparring her a glance

Good boy

"What about you babies? Want to have some fun with us?" The black haired girl asks Azrael and Ezra who are playing with my hands, looking at me.

"Hey love, I don't think they want your number, take a hint." I tell both of them calmly, sending them a fake smile

As if just now noticing me, they both look at me and glare. Seeing them playing with my hands she crosses her arms in front of her "Who are you bitch? No one was asking or talking to you, so just mind your own fucking business cunt." She warns me, waving her finger in my face

The guys stand up from their seats glaring hard at the girls, who take a step back. I give them a look that says 'It's okay, I'll handle this.' they all sit back down while I stand in front of her

Grabbing the girls fingers I bend it backwards making her scream. No one's on this side of the dinner except us, so no one sees us.

I push her and she lands on her hands catching herself.

Seeing people run over to our side I put on an act. "Oh my god, are you okay?" I ask her crouching down to her height on the floor

"What happened?" a lady asks wearing the dinners uniform. "She got up from her seat and fell, I think she broke her fingers from catching herself." I say acting concerned

Looking back I see the guys smirking at me, I give them a small smile and look back at the girls

"No I didn't this bitch pushed me!" She yells, but I put on a confused look

"What are you talking about? I didn't push you." I tell her acting innocent, seeing the other people bought my acting they help her up and make their way to the entrance

"She pushed me!! That bitch pushed me!" She yells walking to the doors

"Do you have evidence that she pushed you?" The lady asks her, the other girl stands there looking down at her feet.

Not getting an answer they leave, I seat back down and they all kiss me on the lips making me smile.

"That was hot." Ezra says putting one arm around my shoulder pulling me closer to him

"Yeah I can agree with that, damn the things you do to me Eden.. .The things you do." Ace says shaking his head, I smile at him.

"Proud of you love, now let's get these milkshakes shall we?" Azrael asks getting the menu out

That was fun!

•*❀☾❀*•

• *~▫• *~▫• *~▫• *~▫• *~*▫• *~▫• *~▫•

Hi.

Thank you for 2.96k, I love you all!

And thank you for the votes. <3

Bye.

•. 23 .•

 Warning this chapter is a bit Steamy in it x

Azrael's Pov-

It's been two weeks since Eden's gone to the hospital she didn't tell us what's wrong so in the mean time, we didn't touch her because we wanted to make sure she was okay, and we didn't hurt her.

Though we've been craving for her touch, we didn't touch her.

The guys are out running errands last minute, leaving me and Eden home alone. I'm glad our office is at home, and not at some big ass building.

Right now I'm in the office trying to sort things out with the ball that's coming up in a few days, and people we need to keep an eye out for, and other shit. I've been busy these past months, and now the paper work is slowly catching up to me.

All this paper work is stressing me out so much, I need a break from all this shit.

I sigh closing my laptop leaning back into my chair, closing my eyes.

A few minutes goes by the door to my office opens, making me open my eyes. I see Eden standing there in a small silk dress, with her hair tied up. Fuck she's beautiful

"Hey love, you okay?" I ask her softly, she walks closer and straddles my lap.

"Yes I'm okay, are you okay?" She asks me, putting her hands on my shoulders gently squeezing them. "I'm okay, just work stressing me out is all." I tell her honestly, leaning into her touch

"Don't overwork yourself." She tells me getting more comfortable in my lap

I grow hard at the feeling of her hot pussy just above my covered cock, her fingers run through my hair making me close my eyes leaning my head back again.

Feeling her trail wet kisses down my neck I sigh at the feeling. Finding my sweet spot I groan, putting my hands on her ass hold it in my palms. Jesus her ass is everything, and her tits, fuck-

She starts to grind on my dick, in slow circles. I lift my hips to meet her, we both moan at the feeling.

"Be careful, my love." I whisper in her ear, making her shiver

"What if I don't want to be careful?" She asks me, looking at me with her big doe eyes full of lust and heat "Take off your underwear." I demand, she's quick to follow. When it's off she steps out of it, making it pool around her feet.

"Good girl." I praise, she quietly moans in return

"Take my cock out." I tell her, her hands go to my belt unbuckling it, when she does she unbuttons my pants, unzipping me.

Pulling down my pants until it's mid thigh she pulls my boxers down making my dick slap my stomach.

She straddles me again, rubbing her sweet wet pussy all up and down my dick, I sigh at the feeling. But I want to be inside her already.

"Stop tease baby." I say looking at her through hooded eyes

She stop and smirks, I reach over to my desk drawer to get a condom. Getting it out she stops me, shaking her head. "No, no more condoms." She says, I'm sorry what?

No more condoms? Did I hear that right?

"I'm sorry what?" I ask her in disbelief

"I...I got birth control, that's why I went to the hospital, to get birth control. I didn't trust the pill one, so I got the IUD and let me tell you that hurt like a bitch." She whispers the last part, stroking my cheeks

"Are you all healed up? What's the doctors name?" I ask her, feeling anger because she got hurt

"It's okay, I'm all healed up. I just didn't want to say anything. But is it okay if we use no condoms?" She asks me rubbing my arms up and down, "Are you sure?" I ask looking up at her

"Yes I'm sure, we don't have to if you don't want to." She tells me making me smile"No I want to, I'm just making sure." I tell her giving her a kiss

"I need to be inside you now." I whisper against her lips

She grabs my dick in her hand lining me up with her entrance, sinking herself down on my cock I'm met her warm tight heat. I couldn't help the groan escaping my lips.

Fuck this feels good, it's been so long since I've had sex.

I groan, her and my breathing uneven. She's half away down "I can't, too much, it won't fit." She says, breathing hard, with her eyes closed

"All of it." I demand looking at her in the eyes

"I can't, it's too much." Putting her head on my shoulder, I stroke her hair kissing her head.

"I'll help it's okay, you can do it." I say "Be a good girl for me okay?" She nods giving me a kiss on the lips

Putting my hands on her hips, I push her down on my cock even more, filing her up. She moans throwing her head back, fucking hot.

"Good girl" I praise kissing her neck, her breathing picks up, she nods and starts moving up and down, with me guiding her hips.

I groan into her neck, letting her set her own pace I enjoy the view. Her head thrown back, covered breast in my face I drag down the straps of her dress and letting it pool around her waist. Her beautiful perky breast that I love come into view, my mouth watering at the site. I take one nipple in my mouth, sucking it, biting it, letting it go with a pop.

Giving her other nipple the same attention.

She rides me faster making me moan around her breast, my cock sliding in and out of her tight heat.

Looking down I see where we're connecting it almost pushes me to the edge.

"God you fucking hot." I moan into her neck, sucking at it.

She tilts her head to the side to give me space, moving her hips back and forth rubbing her clit on me. I rub her clit with my thumb, making her shake in my hold, my baby's sensitive.

I thrust my hips up to meet hers making our skin slap.

"Oh fuck." I groan, throwing my head back closing my eyes. She does this thing with her hips like going in circles, and fuck it feels fucking good.

"Azrael" she moans biting my neck

Never have I ever had someone bite my neck while having sex, but hey there's always a first time for everything right?

I rub her clit harder, making her clench around me in a tight hold.

'I shouldn't do it.''Don't do it Azrael, don't!''Do it!''No''Fucking do it!''Ah fuck it.'

Taking my index finger and middle finger, I slide it to where we're connected.

She's taking me so good, bouncing on my cock making both of us chase our orgasms. I stop moving my hips, while she continues I slide my two fingers into her tight pussy, along side my dick.

"Ah fuck!" She moan loudly panting hard, groaning into my neck.

I start moving my hips with my fingers in her pussy at the same time, fucking hell. My breathing quickens, she clenches around me making me see black spots.

With my other hand I move her hips more faster against mine. Making both of us a moaning and panting mess.

"Fuck you feel so fucking good." I moan kissing her hard, our tongues fighting. I bite her lip drawing a bit of blood, she moans while I release her lip.

Looking up at her she tastes the blood, looking down at me she attacks my lips making me groan. The metallic taste filling my senses, I kiss her rougher trying not to moan at her pussy clenching around me.

Sweat covering both of us.

I take my fingers out of her pussy, leaving my dick inside her. Getting up from my seat I throw everything off my desk, and put her down on it kissing her still.

Unbuttoning my dress shirt I leave it open, she reaches up and runs her fingers on my chest, going to the back she scratches when I thrust even harder wrapping her legs around me, her heels of her feet hitting my ass.

Feeling my balls tighten I moan throwing my head back, gripping her hips harder.

"You close?" I ask her breathlessly, trying to catch my breath

She nods frantically biting her fingers "Words amore mio!" I demand pulling her fingers away from her mouth

"Yes I'm close...so close." At that she clenches around my cock, I moan at the feeling.

"Me too baby, me too." I pant leaning down to capture her lips, grabbing both her breast in my hands I squeeze both, pinching it.

She arches her back, tugging my hair bringing me into her more.

"Faster." She says tugging my hair, arching her back. Eyes closed mouth open.

I pick up the pace, pounding into her relentlessly. She moans loudly cumming all over my dick.

"That's right cum all over my cock." I say, a few more thrusts my body shudders over hers as I cum inside her milking her insides with my cum.

"Holy fuck Eden."

She wraps her arms around my neck, as I collapse on top of her. Careful not to put all my weight on her. Both of us breathing hard, trying to catch our breath.

Running her nails up and down my back, I relax more into her.

That was the best sex I've had, I'm not even lying.

After a few minutes of us laying here on top of my desk she speaks "I didn't think our first time would be here, on your desk." She laughs

I love her laugh.

I laugh lightly into her neck, giving her neck one last kiss before kissing her lips passionately.

Backing away from her I pick up my pants buttoning it back up, before turning to her helping her back into her dress.

"Come on baby, hold on we gotta get you to the shower." I say calmly picking her up

Wrapping her legs around me tightly, she lays her head on my shoulders gently sucking my neck. Yup I definitely have hickeys

"Are you okay, did I hurt you anywhere?" I ask worried trying to distract myself from her sucking on and kissing my neck

"No, you didn't hurt me. I liked it." She tells me, looking at me in the eyes as I make our way to the bathroom.

She kisses me lightly and puts her head back into my shoulder.

"You guys make me feel safe and loved, thank you for caring for me and liking me the way I am." She whispers against my neck, making my heart rate pick up.

I smile softly even though she can't see me

"We'll always like you love, always." I tell her kissing her head

We'll always like you, and keep you safe. Always.

•. 24 .•

Eden's Pov-

"Azrael put me down!" I yell hitting his back, ever since me and Azrael had sex he's been more clingy now. Actually they've all been clingy, but I can't complaining. It's cute

We showered together, got dressed, brushed our teeth and now we're here, going to the living room.

"No." He simply replies smacking my ass

He walks downstairs and oh, it looks like I'm about to fall off his shoulder from this angle. I grab hold his waist tightly, thinking about it I smack his ass.

"Oh you have a fat ass, can I squeeze it?" I ask "No" ah damn- Since I can't do that I'll do something else than

Pinch

"Did you just pinch my ass?" He asks me looking over his shoulder, I shrug

A few seconds later I scream as I get tossed on the couch, Ezra and Ace looking at us with a look of amusement.

'Hi angel''Hey darling'

They both reply at the same time, I smile at them. "Okay so what did you want to ask me?" I ask all of them, they all look at each other eyes saying 'You say it'

"Okay so we wanted to know if you wanted to come to the ball that's coming up in a few days." Azrael says keeping eyes contact with me

"Sounds like fun, I'll go. I've never been to a ball before. Can we look at dresses? I need to find one." I tell them, they all nod

"Let's go right now, since we have nothing else to do. Well we do have stuff to do, but I just want to take a break from the work." Azrael sighs looking at the ceiling.

"Yay, let's go." I get up and go to Aces room to get dressed, since I have some clothes in here. I put on black lace corset top with blue jeans, with black boots, forgetting a jacket because it's hot as fuck outside.

"Okay let's go, you guys ready?" I ask them once I get down to the living room seeing they're waiting

They all stare at me, well more like my boobs. "You can see it later, right now let's go." I say walking away from them. They quickly jump off the couch and follow me outside

Azrael gets inside the car, while I get inside the passenger side. Ace and Ezra get into the back seats.

"Yay, let's go." I say excitedly

•*❀☽❀*•

•*❀☽❀*•

"Do you want us to see the dress?" Ace asks me as we walk into the dress store, and let me tell you...This store has so many beautiful dresses that I've seen, I don't know how I'm going to pick!

Should I let them see the dress I'll pick? No, I want it to be a surprise, I also have to look for some lingerie to go with the dress underneath.

So I'll have them stay outside the stores, yes that's good.

"I want it to be a surprise." I tell them, they all smirk and nod.

"Alright darling, we'll be outside waiting for you to be done. Okay?" Ace says giving my lips a kiss, the other to doing the same.

But Ezra tries kissing me harder, while Ace and Azrael try to drag him away. I smile into the kiss and let him go, he pouts making me laugh. They drag him away and I turn to look at all the dresses.

Pretty! Alright let's do this.

•*❀☽❀*•

I've been in this store for an hour and half, I've tried on so many dresses on, they were all beautiful dresses. One stuck out to me, so I picked it.

Walking outside the store with my dress in hand I see the guys eating some ice cream.

Seeing me walking towards them, Azrael gets up from his seat and takes the dress out my hands, while Ezra pulls out a chair for me to sit in. Before I sit down Ace hand me my ice cream which is cookies and cream. Yummy.

I lick the ice cream, and take a seat beside them at the table and enjoy my ice cream.

Feeling ice cream on the corner of my lips, I take my finger and wipe it off seeing ice cream on it I suck on my finger. Can't waste it.

I look up and see all their eyes trained on my lips, looking at me with lust swimming in their eyes. They lick the lips while staring at my mouth, so I decide to tease them.

Giving my ice cream a nice long lick, I take some into my mouth and lick my lips. Letting out a small quiet moan, they all adjust in their seats making me smile.

I get up from my seat and they follow, I finish the last bit of my ice cream, throw the wrapper away for the cone.

They throw theirs away and follow me around the mall, seeing the lingerie store come into view I turn to look at them. Seeing they're already looking at me.

"I'll be back, I need to go into a store alone. Don't look okay? Stay here, I'll be back." I tell them, they all nod and I walk off

"Be careful Eden." Azrael tells me sternly, I give them all a big smile and make my way over to the store

"Welcome in, is there anything you need help with today?" The lady asks me as soon as I walk in, I tell her what I'm looking for and she gives me a sly smile.

"We've got exactly what you're looking for, follow me." She tells me, walking towards the back

Let's get this over with.

I sigh and walk out the store with the bag in hand, I asked for a plain bag that didn't have the logo or anything on so they didn't see where I went.

I start walking back looking for them only to see them standing where I left them. I shake my head and smile walking towards them.

They're all looking around the mall like lost puppies. Cute.

They see me walking back to them and seeing me walking towards them they all smile widely. "Why are you guys still here? I thought you would've gone back to the food court or something." I ask looking up at them

"Because you told us to stay here." Ezra says walking to bringing me into a bone crushing hug

The other two walk over to us, and join in the hug. I can't breathe, but I feel safe so it's okay.

They all kiss my head letting me go. "Where did you go?" Azrael asks looking me with a confused look

"I would tell you, but that's for you to find out, and for me to know." I tell him, we walk to the shoe store, they all look at different shelves for heels.

Seeing a really gorgeous pair I walk up to it and look at it in my hands, admiring it.

This is it, this is the one.

"You want this love?" Azrael asks wrapping his arms around my waist, giving my neck a kiss making me sigh at the feeling

I nod and turn around to show him, "Those are beautiful baby, I'm sure you'll look gorgeous in it, along with your dress." He says giving me a kiss, Ace and Ezra walk over and look at the heels in my hand. They smile at me and we walk to the register to pay.

After about 5 minutes of arguing with Ace that I should pay and not him, I give in letting him pay. He smirks handing the lady the card, she looks at all of them with lust in her eyes making me sigh.

They're hit, I get it. But do they always have to stare?

She starts to wrap up my shoes while looking at all of them still, her movements slowly stopping. Her eyes travel up and down each one of them, mainly stopping at their dick, and forearms that display their tattoos. She rubs her thighs together biting her lip.

This bitch!

Walking up behind Ace, I stand behind him wrapping my arms around his waist making him turn around smirking down at me. Azrael and Ezra walk up to us, Azrael puts his hands on my waist holding me while standing beside me on my right side. Ezra puts his hands on my shoulders pulling me back into him, Ezra leans down tucking his head in my neck giving it a kiss. While Azrael kiss the opposite side of my neck Ezra's kissing, Ace on the other hand is kissing me.

They both kiss my neck, while I kiss Ace running my hands through his hair.

I open my eyes still kissing Ace, and look at her straight in the eyes smirking at her.

He face is all red, while she's standing there with wide eyes, and open mouth. Cold sweat breaks out on her forehead seeing her slowly turn pale.

I pull away from their hold and grab the bag, and Aces card handing it back to him. I smirk at the lady, and we all walk out.

"You hungry angel?" Ezra asks me intertwining our fingers as we walk back to the car

"Can we get Mexican food?" I ask them as we get inside the car after putting the bags in the back

"Anything you want." He replies coming between the two seats giving me a kiss on the lips, before sitting back in his seat.

The balls in a few days, I can't wait for them to see what I bought.

•*❀☽❀*•

•. 25 •

A/N; I'm sorry for the late update!

Eden's Pov-

It's been two days since I got my dress, and the guys won't leave me alone about it. The ball is tomorrow, and I'm so excited to go. There's gonna be a lot of people though and that's gonna suck.

I'm gonna throw myself off a bridge.

I've seen that in movies, it looks boring. Yet peaceful at the same time.

"Eden come on!" Ace yells catching everyone's attention at the beach. Rolling my eyes I sigh and began walking over to where he is "I'm coming I'm coming."

"You walk slow." Ace says looking down at me

"Says the one who complains about his knees hurting, you old fart." I say looking up at him, why does he have to be so tall?

I mean I'm not complaining, we love tall men.

We continue walking meeting up with Ezra and Azrael, they wanted to take me to the beach to go for a swim, but no one told me how much people would be here.

Seeing girls look at them like they're something to eat, trying to catch their attention but they're to busy looking at me. Hahaaaa sucker!

Sitting down they all give me a kiss on my forehead 3000....

I just want to know who in the family gave me the huge forehead, I just want to talk.

"You coming in? Let's go." Azrael says rubbing sunscreen on my thighs while Ace is rubbing screen on my back, and Ezra rubs my arms.

I sigh at the feeling, this feels good.

They already have sunscreen on, so might as well go in the water.

"Let's go" I say getting up from the chair with the help of Azrael who almost pulls my arms out of its socket. So caring, my caring boy.

Ah fun times, fun times!

I take off my towel from around me dropping it to the ground, revealing my black two piece set. Looking up I see all their attention on me, more like my boobs. Perverts

I cross my arms in front of my chest seeing all of them smirk at me. I smile and continue walking towards them.

Ace walks towards me seeing a glint of mischief in his eyes I back away slowly. He runs after me while I try to run the opposite way. "Come here Eden!" Ace yells coming closer to me.

I take a few more steps before I fell his arm around my waist picking me up.

"Put me down!" I yell at Ace while hitting his back, looking around I see a group of girls giving me dirty looks.

You wish that was you huh?

Seeing him walk into the water I start to move around more, not prepared to get thrown in.

Not even a second later I'm getting tossed into the ocean like a rag doll. Coming back up to the surface I inhale a deep breath while coughing, because some water got into my nose.

I hate when that happens.

I look to my right and see all three of them coming towards me, looking beautiful as always.

"Are you okay? I'm sorry I didn't mean to throw you that hard." Ace exclaimed with a worried look on his face.

"I'm okay, I'm fine, it's okay. Let's go get something to drink, I'm thirsty." I say walking back to shore with them right behind me

I got thrown in like a rag doll, so I got to prepare myself this time. Gotta catch a breather, and go back out there, for now I don't want to die getting thrown around by these giants.

As I'm walking I see a group of guys walking around carrying a volleyball and drinks.

Looks like fun!

All of a sudden I'm getting picked up and thrown back into the water, by a grumpy looking Azrael. What's his problem?

"Why'd you do that?" I ask trying not to cough

"You we're looking at those guys." Azrael says looking anywhere but me

"I was looking at the volleyball, not them." I stated walking back to them, or at least trying to the waters to heavy around my legs

"You promise?" Ezra asks looking at me with an extended hand towards me

"Yes I promise now let's go!" I said taking his hand

Finally making it back to our stuff, which is surprising still here I pick up my water opening it before drinking half of it

As I'm drinking some, I see the group of guys looking at me. One of them points at me smiling.

Seeing I'm still looking at them Ace squeezes my water bottle, making it to splash all over me and causing some to go into my nose making me cough.

Ouch this burns my nose

"Eden I'm sorry, you were looking at them. I panicked so I did that." Ace says quickly while putting his hands on my shoulder, while I wipe my eyes

These guys are trying to kill me...lovely!

Once I'm done calming down, I get up seeing there's a ice cream stand not to far from us.

"Where are you going?" Azrael asks getting in a sitting position

"I'm going to get some ice cream I'll be back." I tell them, walking towards the ice cream stand

"Hi there, what can I get you today?" The girl asks giving me the most heart warming smiling, making me smile back

"Hi, I'd like to get one cone. Two scoops of strawberry please." I tell her, and focus on her scooping the ice cream

A few seconds later she's done "That'll be $2.50 please" she tells me handing me my ice cream, yay!

I hand her the money and start to lock my ice cream walking off when all of a sudden I felt a tap on my shoulder

"Hey pretty lady" I hear as I turn around, oh it's the guy that was pointing at me earlier

"Can I help you?" I ask as politely as possible, he's giving off a weird vibe

"Can I have your number?" He asks while looking at my lips with a lustful look

"No, no I have a boyfriend." I tell him as i start to back away, but he reaches forward to grab my hand but I retract it quickly.

"What's wrong? It's okay he doesn't have to know doll. I'm sure your brothers don't mind if I still you for awhile." He smirks trying to reach out again

Did...did he just say my brother? Oh my-

Feeling myself get irritated I push my ice cream in his face, breaking the cone.

"Yo what the fuck is wrong with you? Are you fucking mad? Do you know who my father is you fucking bitch?" He yells rubbing the ice cream out of his eyes

"No I don't, and I don't care." I say as I'm turning away from him, but only to be met with a chest.

Looking up I see a very angry Ezra, Ace, and Azrael, uh oh.

"What did you just call our girlfriend?" Ezra says, putting his arm around my waist dragging me behind me, not even taking his eyes off the guy in front of him.

"Y-your girlfriend?" The guy says looking at us in disbelief

"Did he fucking stutter? He asked what did you just call our girlfriend?" Ace says starring at the guy dead in the eyes making him shift on his feet

"N-nothing, I'm sorry uh miss. I gotta get going now." He says running away, haha pussy

My gosh I cuss a lot because of these three men right here, mhm I need to go to church.

"Hey Love are you okay?" Azrael asks looking at me with concern

Nodding I say "Yeah I'm okay, he wouldn't leave me alone. So I threw my ice cream in his face. Hope he likes strawberry."

They all smile down at me.

"Alright stay here." Ezra says walking away

Confused I look at where he's going, he goes to the ice cream stand. A minute later he comes back with a strawberry ice cream.

My heart!

"Here you go angel, don't throw this one." He jokes handing me the ice cream, I smile and kiss his cheek

Azrael and Ace lean down looking at me, I smile and kiss their cheeks as well.

This is nice.

CPSIA information can be obtained
at www.ICGtesting.com
Printed in the USA
LVHW052023090123
736787LV00009B/272